A Winter Wedding

A Lord For All Seasons
Book 4

Nadine Millard

ARE YOU SIGNED UP FOR DRAGONBLADE'S BLOG?

You'll get the latest news and information on exclusive giveaways, exclusive excerpts, coming releases, sales, free books, cover reveals and more.

Check out our complete list of authors, too!

No spam, no junk. That's a promise!

Sign Up Here

www.dragonbladepublishing.com

Dearest Reader;

Thank you for your support of a small press. At Dragonblade Publishing, we strive to bring you the highest quality Historical Romance from some of the best authors in the business. Without your support, there is no 'us', so we sincerely hope you adore these stories and find some new favorite authors along the way.

Happy Reading!

CEO, Dragonblade Publishing

Additional Dragonblade books by Author Nadine Millard

A Lord For All Seasons Series
A Springtime Scandal (Book 1)
Midsummer Madness (Book 2)
A Forgotten Fall (Book 3)
A Winter Wedding (Book 4)

Also from Nadine Millard
A Duke Never Tells (Novella)

Prologue

"SOPHIA, YOU DO know that you cannot spend the entire evening with the horses?"

Sophia Templeworth spun around at the sound of her sister's voice behind her. "You scared me half to death," she groused at Hope who was eyeing her speculatively across the darkened stables. She hated when Hope got that look on her face. Like she was trying to root out everyone's secrets. Well, she'd have a hard time finding any in here, because Sophia didn't have secrets. And she certainly had never made any secret of the fact that she preferred the company of horses to humans.

"I don't see why not, in any case," she continued a little tartly. "Cheska and Adam have already escaped. If they're not going to stay at their own wedding, I don't see why I should have to."

Hope opened her mouth to respond but froze for a moment before shrugging her shoulders. "That's fair enough," she said, and Sophia smiled gratefully at her older sister. As the youngest of the four Templeworth girls, she didn't feel as though they always took her opinions and feelings on matters into consideration.

Elodie, now the Viscountess of Brentford, had always acted as though she knew best in any given situation, which was accurate, actually, but still sometimes annoying. Hope, now the Countess of Claremont, cared not a whit for how she *should* act in company, hence why she'd conceded to Sophia's point. And Francesca, who'd been the Marchioness of Heywood for about

1

three hours now, would have laughed outright at any attempt to tell her what to do.

"But you might want to rethink the gown, dear," Hope continued with a grin. "I'm not sure that Parisian satin and horseflesh go all that well together."

Sophia rolled her eyes, but a smile tugged at her lips. Indeed, she couldn't imagine how odd it looked to be bedecked in diamonds and satins whilst rubbing down the flank of a horse. It was just that her animals, her stables, were her favorite spot. When being sociable and mannerly became too much for her, which it almost always did, she could spend hours with her horses, and the world returned to rights. And since she'd been blessed with three brothers-in-law who had exceptionally good taste in horseflesh, she'd been spoiled with access to their mounts. Indeed, she'd spent so much time with Adam's horse recently that she hadn't really paid attention to him seducing her sister under her very nose.

Still, Cheska never would have been seduced against her will, Sophia assured herself. And just like Elle and Hope, Francesca was sickeningly in love with her husband. Sophia couldn't understand any of them. She loved Christian, Gideon, and Adam. She loved how much they adored her sisters and how she knew they'd never let any harm befall them. But honestly, she couldn't imagine ever spending enough time with anyone to fall in love. People, except for a very select few, invariably bored her senseless or annoyed her to no end. And horses never did.

"I feel it prudent to warn you, though, that Mama won't be long hunting you down. Come on, Sophia," Hope coaxed. "Just dance one dance with a gentleman, and I'll cover for you while you make a run for it."

Hope would, too, Sophia knew. In fact, it felt like the Templeworth girls spent their lives covering for each other's escapes. Even Elodie! Though that had been just one time, and she'd ended up marrying Christian after she'd stowed away in his carriage. Even so, it did seem to be something the sisters did quite frequently.

"Who am I to dance with?" she grumbled, though she still dutifully shuffled toward the exit of the stables. "Dr. Pearse who's nursing his broken heart over losing Francesca and her ankles to Adam? Or perhaps the pig farmer who's tried to win Elodie, you, *and* Cheska? Tell me that a horse isn't a better option than either of them."

Hope laughed as she pulled Sophia's hand into the crook of her arm and marched them both back to the house. "What about Adam's friend, the duke? He is positively delicious! And that Scottish brogue of his? A dance with him would be no bad thing."

For some reason, Sophia felt a little on edge at the mention of the Duke of Farnshire. He'd come for the wedding, invited by Adam since he'd claimed that the duke was the only person whose company he'd been able to stomach after the war. And to his credit, the handsome duke had seemed genuinely thrilled that Adam had fallen in love with Cheska and was on the way to healing. Sophia didn't really know much about Adam's journey, save that he spoke often about how Cheska had brought him back to life. She didn't feel as though she should pry.

"I'm not dancing with a duke in front of Mama," Sophia said stoutly as she dragged her mind away from the duke's black-as-night hair and deep, chocolate-brown eyes. "I don't even want to think on how she'd let her imagination run wild.

"Hmm. You may have a point," Hope said thoughtfully. "She does seem rather zealous about getting you married off."

"Yes, she does. And I blame you entirely. Well, you, Elodie, and Francesca. Why did you all have to go falling in love and having babies? Especially with wealthy peers of the realm? You've given the woman notions, for goodness' sake!"

Hope's laugh did nothing to improve Sophia's vaguely sour mood. "Sorry." Her sister offered, though of course, she wasn't sorry at all. And why would she be?

Gideon absolutely adored her, and she him. Their children were as beautiful as their parents. Their lives together were almost perfect. It was the same for Elodie and Christian and would doubtless be the same for Cheska and Adam. But Sophia already knew that she'd never experience that type of love. Mostly because she didn't want to. She was genuinely content, perfectly happy in fact, to be single and left alone with her horses.

"One dance," Hope offered, her tone conciliatory. "With whomever you choose as long as he only has two legs," she continued with a wink, and Sophia grinned in response. "Then I'll keep Mama distracted long enough for you to slip out and away from ankle-loving doctors and odious pig farmers."

"Deal," Sophia said quickly. "I suppose if I *do* dance with the duke, it will gain Mama's approval for at least a few days."

"That's the spirit," Hope drawled sarcastically, and they hurried back to the house, arms still entwined.

Chapter One

DEVON BLAKE, DUKE of Farnshire, frowned at the darkening sky as he drew his stallion to a halt in front of Heywood Manor, the country house of his old friend Adam Fairchild. It had been over a year since he'd attended Adam's wedding here. He'd never forget his shocked delight at receiving the news that Adam had not only started to put his demons to rest, but that he'd found a woman he loved with all his heart. And better yet, a woman who knew all his darkness and loved him for it.

Devon knew now more than ever how important it was to have someone in your life that you could lean on through difficult times. Knew because when his own world had been flipped on its head, he'd realized just how alone he truly was.

There were lots of things that he'd remembered about that visit to Halton, where he'd now come to spend Christmastide with Adam and his lovely marchioness. The curiously endearing oddity of the village folk. The beauty and wit of Adam's formidable wife, matched only by that of her sisters. There'd been a viscountess, he remembered. And a countess. And then there'd been the younger one, the horse-mad brunette who'd danced just once with him and then disappeared for the rest of the celebration.

She'd been a strange one. Beautiful and audacious like her sisters, but very obviously uninterested in anyone and anything around her.

Devon had felt his curiosity piqued by the diminutive Templeworth girl, yet any attempts to see her again or even get a decent conversation out of her had been met with vague irritation or in the case of the latter, outright refusal. Devon had stayed in Halton for a few days after Adam had left on his honeymoon, given that traveling back to the wilds of Scotland, back to his two young charges, required a lot more organizing than he'd been used to at the time.

As his thoughts returned to the children. Devon turned his head to peer into his lacquered carriage, the one he'd rode close to even when he'd wanted to just give Aengus his head and gallop through the countryside. But he wouldn't leave the children alone, even with their sour-faced nanny accompanying them inside the coach and his team of footmen surrounding it.

They still weren't entirely comfortable being away from home for too long. Hell, they still weren't entirely comfortable with *him*. And the feeling was mutual. It wasn't that he didn't love the children, indeed he had grown to love them as much as if they were biologically his. It was just that when they'd come to him, fatherhood had been a distant imagining, something he knew he'd have to succumb to in the future. He'd never expected to have his poor sister's children thrust upon him in the aftermath of her death.

Heather's husband had died in a tragic hunting accident while she'd been pregnant with her daughter. The grief had brought on an early labor, the physician had told him of that awful, fateful night. And with the complications of the delivery, he hadn't been able to save her. He'd barely been able to save the babe. But wee Heather, named for her dear Mama, was made of stern Scottish stock, and had come on in leaps and bounds during her infancy, quickly catching up to her older brother. Of course, Devon hadn't known any of this until he'd returned from overseeing a new business interest in the West Indies.

The letters sent hadn't reached him given that he'd been traveling from one obscure place to another. By the time he'd come home, it had all been over and done with and a year had passed. Heather had been buried, his mother had been mired in grief, and he was the terrifyingly unprepared guardian of two, tiny children.

Now a year later, he, Heather, and Finn managed to rub along well together. Heather was already a little tearaway at just three years old, and Finn, though he was a little more serious than a lad of six should be, no longer awoke from nightmares screaming for his mother.

He made eye contact with Mrs. McCluddy, who signaled that both children were sleeping. The journey from his main seat in Scotland to Halton was long and arduous. But when Adam and Francesca had invited him to stay for the Yuletide Season, he'd thought it might be nice for the children, especially since his mother still didn't like to celebrate holidays. Adam had written that the entirety of Francesca's intimidatingly madcap family were descending on Halton for the festivities along with their brood of offspring, and Devon had wanted Finn and Heather to have playmates to enjoy their presents with.

Last year, the Templeworths had still been in mourning after their father's death, so there'd been little in the way of celebrations, Adam had explained. This year, he meant to give his wife a Christmastide to remember. Especially since he hadn't been able to throw her an apparently much-beloved harvest fest, given that the family had been in the end stages of their mourning period. Either way, the children would enjoy whatever activities Adam had planned.

These days, he felt an almost permanent nagging worry that Heather and Finn weren't having a good childhood. That he wasn't making enjoyable memories for them. That they'd look back on it and think him a failure. It didn't help that Mrs. McCluddy was a veritable dragon who had no patience for Heather's wildness or Finn's shyness. He really needed to get around to a better solution for them all. The widow was getting on in years and simply didn't have the energy for young children anymore.

He'd only kept her on as their nanny because when he'd returned to Scotland his mother had already hired her, and he hadn't gotten around to finding something better. Running a duchy the size of Farnshire was no mean feat, and Devon never seemed to have enough time for the poor mites, to find them someone who wouldn't just tolerate them but love them as they deserved. They needed someone younger, someone more spirited and kinder than Mrs. McCluddy. They needed a mother.

The sigh that escaped him felt as though it came from the depths of his soul. Marriage was just another inconvenience that he'd have to deal with at some point. Another job that he didn't relish having to do. He had no notions of love. A duke rarely had the luxury of such things in any case. He needed to marry for the title. And now, for the children.

Bloody hell. He'd come here to get away from his problems, not sit stewing on them.

He was about to dismount and hand Aengus over to a waiting stable lad when the sound of thundering hooves rent the air, and he turned in his saddle to see a huge horse racing up the gravel driveway. He didn't need the rider to come any closer to know it was Sophia Templeworth. If the long, chestnut hair flying out behind her hadn't been a dead giveaway, the lady's riding would have been.

He'd only seen her ride once before last year, and even then, it had been obvious that she had one of the best seats he'd ever seen. In a man or woman. Her command of the beast beneath her was smoothly impressive. And the fact that she rode astride, clad not in dainty skirts but in skintight breeches wasn't at all surprising, especially since Adam had told him of the chit's obsession with horses.

She would love the stables at Farnshire, he thought suddenly. He'd invested a fortune in them over the years, being an avid horse lover himself. It would be nice, he realized, to show them off to someone who would truly appreciate them.

He watched wordlessly as her mount veered off the main gravel driveway and around the back of the house. To the stables, he remembered. She was obviously here often enough to use the house as her own.

The door to the manor house opened, and there was a sudden flurry of activity as servants came toward them followed by a smiling Adam and, Devon noticed in surprised delight, a pregnant Francesca.

The difference in his friend was astonishing. Adam didn't just look at peace but utterly contented. Deliriously happy and proud. And Devon was glad for his friend, he thought as he reached out to clasp Adam's hand in a warm greeting. Nobody deserved a happy family more than his old friend. Nobody, perhaps, but the two innocent babes asleep inside his carriage.

Chapter Two

"**D**ID YOU KNOW there was a carriage outside the house?" Sophia had barely gotten the question out when Adam leapt to his feet, reaching out to help Francesca to stand before they both hurried from the room. Cheska's belly was barely rounded yet, and Adam had been acting as though she was completely infirm ever since she'd told him she was with child. At least according to Cheska, who had been writing to Sophia diligently ever since she'd moved away to Adam's main seat at Heywood Abbey.

As usual, when Sophia thought of Cheska living so far away, she got that aching pang in her belly. She had missed Elle when she'd gone, and Hope, too, of course. But Francesca's leaving hit her the hardest of all, because she really was the last one standing now. The one left behind. And though she didn't resent her sisters' happiness, she didn't like how lonely she was without them.

And now that they were out of mourning, she had to face the harsh reality of what her life was, of who she was going to be from here on in. The spinster sister relying on the kindness of Christian, Gideon, or Adam. Likely all three. For as humiliating as it was, the fact was that their father had left them broke after years of mismanagement of his already modest estate.

If Elle, Hope, and Cheska hadn't fallen in love with wealthy peers, they'd be even worse off. But they'd been lucky enough to have three rich gentlemen absolutely besotted with them, so the question of dowries had never really arisen. They'd have taken them with nothing. And by the time he'd passed away, that's precisely what Papa had left for Sophia. Nothing.

Sophia had never worried about a dowry since she'd never intended to marry. Why would she? She'd never met a man who held more than a fleeting interest for her, and as long as she had her horses, she was quite content with her lot in life.

It was only when Papa's will had been read that they'd realized their comfortable existence relied on debts mounting and bills going unpaid. Papa had never cared about his children; it had been obvious in his complete lack of interest or presence in their lives. But to find out that he'd gone to his grave not even caring about what the future might hold for his wife and last daughter had been quite the slap in the face. And Sophia's already complicated feelings around her father had grown even more turbulent. She had loved him, she supposed, because he was her father. But she'd never been sure that he'd loved her. Or any of them.

And of course, the strain of their financial disgrace had come with the added problem of Mama's hysterics. She'd taken to her bed for weeks after the news, and Sophia was left dealing with everything. Thankfully, her sisters had rallied, and Elle in that wonderful, calm way of hers had managed to appease disgruntled servants and merchants. To Sophia's unending shame, Christian, Gideon, and Adam had paid off the staff still owed wages and the local merchants with tabs that had grown eye-wateringly long. Sophia knew she'd never be able to repay them. Quite literally. If she'd been born a man, she could have earned money, but as it was, she was stuck relying on their love for their wives to stay out of destitution.

Of course, almost from the second Mama was out of her dull black and grey clothing, she'd stopped pretending to be a grieving widow who missed her husband and was relishing the idea of moving in with one of her titled daughters.

Sophia managed to smile a bit when she remembered the fights they'd all had about who'd get stuck with Mama. In the end, Christian had decided that he was going to purchase Papa's house, pay off the mortgage, and let Mama and Sophia stay in it. Because he knew, he'd said stoutly brooking no argument, that Elodie would end up folding to guilt and familial duty, that she was too kind-hearted not to let Mama's manipulation work on her. And that he'd end up stuck with his mother-in-law and worse, he'd have to watch Elodie be mistreated forever.

Sophia had always known that Christian was fiercely protective of his viscountess. She hadn't imagined he was protective enough to purchase an entire *house,* but then he'd assured them all, it was as much for him as it was for Elle.

For their own parts, Hope and Cheska hadn't even been sorry to tell him how right he was. Hope had snorted at the very idea of living with Mama again, and Cheska's particularly colorful way with words had left them all in no doubt as to where she stood on the subject.

Sophia tried to shake off her maudlin thoughts. It would be Christmas soon, a holiday that she loved. The whole family would be here. There would be games and music, laughter, and *fun.* Something she didn't really feel she'd had since her sisters had all left and moved on with their lives. Something she hadn't really had at all in the past year. The last time she could remember truly enjoying herself had been at Adam and Francesca's wedding, and that had been fifteen months ago.

Thoughts of the wedding immediately led to thoughts of Adam's friend the duke, and Sophia suddenly realized why the crest on the carriage outside had seemed vaguely familiar. He was here. The Duke of Farnshire. The man with whom she'd danced and then run away because he'd made her feel…odd. That was it. He'd awoken in her a strange, not entirely unpleasant edginess that she'd never experienced before. And it had made her feel so uneasy that she'd simply left Heywood Manor and gone home.

It had been perhaps a bit of an overreaction. And certainly, extremely unsophisticated. But she'd never liked feeling anything other than perfectly in control of herself and her life. And Devon Blake had made her feel decidedly *out* of control. At least in those last moments of the dance when he'd bowed over her hand and then looked up at her with those dark-as-sin eyes and she'd felt—well, she didn't quite know. Something akin to the rush when she made a particularly difficult or dangerous jump on her horse.

The sound of booming voices and footsteps sounded outside, and Sophia knew that Cheska must be returning with her guests. She glanced down at herself, frowning slightly as she imagined Mama's screeching when she found out Sophia had met a duke in muddy breeches with her hair tumbling down her back. Well, it was no matter. She could just lie and say she'd borrowed a gown from Cheska if the subject came up.

The door suddenly burst open, and in charged a tiny whirlwind of sable curls. Sophia's mouth popped open as a little girl skidded to a halt in front of her and stared up at her with the biggest brown eyes she'd ever seen. They reminded Sophia of Elodie's eyes, or Hope's.

"Er, hello," Sophia offered with a smile. "Who..."

"Heather, lass. I told you that you must stay with Mrs. McCluddy."

Sophia felt her eyes widen as the Duke of Farnshire arrived in the doorway, filling it with his giant frame. She'd forgotten just how big he was, but he was truly huge. She remembered that Adam had laughingly referred to Lord Farnshire's Highlander roots when Hope had asked how tall he was and where he'd gotten those shoulders of his. And she remembered Gideon's scowl as he'd pulled his wife proprietarily toward him. But the duke, to his credit, had merely laughed at Hope's outrageousness.

"Oh, forgive me." He moved his eyes from the tiny girl who was running in circles around where Sophia stood, and Sophia felt oddly trapped in his dark gaze. "Miss Templeworth." His bow was perfectly executed and reminded Sophia that she should curtsy, which she hastily did.

"Good afternoon, Your Grace," she said a little stiffly. That strange tension she'd felt around him last year was back, and she found she didn't quite know what to do with herself when he was looking so keenly at her.

The tiny terror at their feet drew to a sudden stop and pulled at Sophia's navy-blue riding jacket. Glad of the chance to break the duke's intense stare, she turned her attention to the child. "Who are you?" the little one asked with the softest Scottish lilt.

Sometimes the duke himself had that twang, Sophia recalled. After their dance, before she'd run from him, he'd asked if she'd like to walk outside, and she'd noticed it then. She opened her mouth to answer the girl, her cheeks heating as she remembered her barmy behavior of ignoring his question and quite simply running away, when Lord Farnshire spoke up again.

"Heather, lass. I've told you that you must wait for people to be introduced to you." Though his tone was patient, Sophia could have sworn that the tot, young as she clearly was, rolled her eyes at the gentle reprimand, and Sophia couldn't help but grin down at the little one. Having lived a life of perpetual eye-rolling and reprimands, she sensed a kindred spirit.

"Sorry, Uncle Devon," came the retort, which sounded as far from sorry as one could be.

Uncle Devon. Of course. Sophia remembered now that the man had two charges, his sister's children, Adam had said. Orphaned whilst the duke had been on the other side of the world. Not usually one for sentimentality, Sophia couldn't help her heart melting just a tiny bit for the tiny girl and the giant man who was frowning down at her as though he didn't quite know what to do with her.

Deciding to spare them both further awkwardness, and because she'd never particularly cared about silly Society rules either, Sophia hunkered down until she was eye level with the little one. "I am Sophia Templeworth," she said with a smile. "This is my sister's house. And you are Heather?"

The little one smiled and nodded then reached out and

grabbed hold of one of Sophia's tumbling curls. "I like your hair," she said bluntly, and Sophia laughed softly, utterly charmed by her. "And I like yours," she answered. "It's almost the same color as mine, see?" She held out the lock that Heather had gripped, then pulled out one of Heather's shorter ones. Indeed, though Heather's hair was sable like her uncles, and Sophia's a rich chestnut with strands of rich burgundy, they were both dark-haired enough that the similarity was there.

Heather squealed with excitement. "Look, Uncle Devon. We almost match."

Sophia looked up at the duke, thinking they'd share an indulgent, conspiratorial smile about the little girl's delight. But when she found his eyes already locked on hers, with some intense emotion darkening their depths to black, she found her smile die and her breath hitch.

She had no idea what she'd done to put that look on his face, to ignite that blazing intensity in his gaze, but whatever it was it scared and intrigued her in equal measure.

Chapter Three

"THERE YOU ARE. Lady Heather, I've told you and told you that you cannot run away from me. A thousand apologies, Your Grace."

Devon managed to pull his gaze from the tableau before him, though it took a surprising amount of effort. He wouldn't even know how to begin to explain his reaction to seeing Sophia Templeworth kneeling beside Heather, putting that wee smile on his niece's face. The picture they painted, the chestnut-haired beauty and his tiny niece, it spoke to something within him, awoke something tender within in his heart.

Christ, he'd forgotten how beautiful Sophia Templeworth was. Even as he turned to face a scowling Mrs. McCluddy, he saw her stand with grace, her sinfully curved body shown to mouth-watering perfection in the tight, riding breeches and fitted jacket. And he saw that glorious hair spilling down her back to her waist. He also saw her narrow those impossibly blue eyes at Mrs. McCluddy, who was scowling fiercely down at Heather.

He really hated the older woman's dourness. He'd oft wondered if it would kill her to bestow a bloody smile on the children every once in a while. He really did need to prioritize pensioning her off. Heather's beaming face when Miss Templeworth had shown her a few moments of kindness proved just how vital it was to get rid of her.

"No apology necessary, Mrs. McCluddy."

"She was doing no harm."

Devon's placating tone was interrupted by Sophia Temple-worth's glacial one, and he turned to see Heather move closer to the lady's side. Just like that. Finn, who'd been hiding behind Mrs. McCluddy's wool skirts peeked his head out, the picture of reserved curiosity.

"Was she, Your Grace?"

"The children's care is my concern as their nanny, Miss—?" Mrs. McCluddy's tone was patronizing and unpleasant, and he saw Miss Templeworth's gaze narrow even more dangerously.

Devon found himself starting between the two women, feeling inexplicably uncomfortable. He was a duke, for God's sake. He wasn't afraid of a chit of a girl or a damned nanny! Especially a nanny who apparently needed to learn her place in more ways than one. Yet he found himself hesitant to upset either woman for fear of his life.

"Sophia, I see you've met Mrs. McCluddy. And the duke's niece. But have you met his nephew? Finn, dear, this is my sister Sophia. Who is *not* about to do battle with another woman in my drawing room."

Devon was slightly ashamed of how relieved he felt at Francesca's outrageous comment, which drew both Sophia and Mrs. McCluddy's attention away from each other and from him. Then he watched in silence once more as the sisters engaged in some sort of war of wills. But eventually Sophia turned her attention to Finn who'd stepped a little further away from the glowering nanny and was gazing curiously up at her.

Devon's heart stuttered yet again as Sophia Templeworth's icy demeanor immediately melted into a soft, welcoming smile as she looked at Finn who was gripping the figurine of a horse in his hand. He never went anywhere without that horse. Devon knew from his mother that the boy's father had owned it as a lad and had passed it down. It was so weathered and scuffed now that Devon was surprised it hadn't yet fallen apart.

He watched Finn's face closely as Sophia Templeworth bent

toward him. Already Francesca had shown the lad such warmth and kindness that it had made Devon feel oddly emotional. Heather had outrun them all to the house, of course, leaving Devon with no choice but to run after the little midge. Yet he had hesitated knowing that Finn would be left with just Mrs. McCluddy. The second he'd seen Adam and Francesca's warmth toward the lad though, he'd been sure that they'd put him at his ease.

Now, he only hoped Sophia Templeworth would do the same. "Hello, Finn," she said softly. When Finn didn't respond, just continuing to stare up at her with those big, solemn eyes of his, Devon made to step in. But to his surprise, Miss Templeworth once again dropped to her haunches until she was eye level with Finn. And God forgive him for the depraved bastard he clearly was, but Devon couldn't help noticing the pull of her tight breeches over her legs and behind at the action. Noticing, and salivating, which was hardly appropriate in the circumstances.

"And who might this be?" She kept her tone light and friendly, even though Finn was giving her nothing in response. "You know, he looks exactly like my horse Hero. He's an old man now, but when he was younger, I could have sworn he could fly."

As closely as Devon was watching, he saw Finn's eyes widen at Miss Templeworth's description of her horse. "Uncle Devon got me a pony," Finn said shyly. "He's called Bracken." He frowned slightly. "I don't think he can fly though."

Sophia Templeworth's laugh was a thing of beauty, and Devon was struck a little dumb by it. But more so by Finn opening up to the lady, giving her a wide, not often seen grin.

"I don't think Hero could really fly either," she whispered conspiratorially to the lad. "But it certainly felt as though he did. But I do know that you have to wait until you're at least as big as Lord Heywood before you can try it. Otherwise, it won't work."

Devon's relief was palpable. He should have picked up on the fact that Finn might attempt something dangerous. But he'd been too busy watching Miss Templeworth to notice that a six-year-old boy might be getting ideas about flying a horse.

Finn cocked his head curiously. "I can get as big as Lord Heywood," he said with careful consideration. "As long as I don't have to get as big as Uncle Devon."

His innocent remark broke the odd tension in the room. The adults laughed, except Mrs. McCluddy, who frowned disapprovingly and set about jostling the children out of the room and up to the nursery to rest. Devon couldn't help but wonder why they'd need to rest after being cooped up in a carriage day in and day out for the days that it took them to travel from Scotland, but as usual, he deferred to Mrs. McCluddy's experience, even if it didn't sit well with him.

He watched their little faces fall when the nanny hurried them from the room, and that gut-wrenching sadness hit him again. Perhaps he didn't speak up enough for them. Perhaps they needed him more than he had imagined. He already knew they needed more than Mrs. McCluddy. Without conscious thought, his eyes were drawn to Miss Templeworth, who was staring after the children, too. Perhaps, he thought, they needed someone like her.

"LORD, WHAT A nasty old trout." Sophia didn't bother to keep her voice down as Cheska led her toward the chaise by the window where they usually sat.

Sophia had grown used to Heywood Manor when Cheska had hurt her ankle, and they'd both stayed here. Cheska so she could recuperate and Sophia so she could be a chaperone. Why anyone had thought that would be a good idea, Sophia didn't know, for she spent her days away from the house with Adam's horses while Adam and Cheska blatantly fell in love under her nose. Still, it had all worked out, and now she was comfortable enough here to treat the place as her own.

In fact, Adam had told her more than once that she could come here whenever she chose, even while he and Francesca where at his main seat. Though he didn't keep horses stabled here, he didn't keep a skeletal staff. And Sophia had taken advantage of his offer so much, especially since her father had died, that the staff treated her as though she were a Heywood, and she felt quite at home in the manor.

Or at least she would have done were it not for the Duke of Farnshire's looming presence. That look he'd given her when she'd been speaking with his niece was still stamped firmly in her mind. Coupled with the way he'd watched so protectively over that shy little boy; well, it was enough to distract a girl. And she didn't want to be distracted by him.

"That's far more polite than anything I would have called her," Cheska agreed as they sat and watched the gentlemen approach. "Your Grace, if I may be bold, why on earth do you put up with it?"

Adam chuckled softly as he took one of the armchairs facing the chaise, leaving the duke to take the other.

"What are you laughing at?" Cheska asked, her tone affronted.

"Nothing, darling. I've just never heard you ask permission to be bold. Or to voice your opinion. Or to care if someone *gave* you permission or not."

Sophia laughed, too, and while Francesca *tried* to look offended, eventually, even she had to smile.

"Fine," she said. "Regardless of whether you give me permission to be bold or not, Lord Farnshire, why on earth do you put up with her?"

Sophia wasn't sure how the duke would react to Cheska's forthrightness. She'd hadn't really spent enough time around him to know what his reaction would be either way. But he laughed, the sound doing funny things to her insides. "The truth is that I do not know why I've put up with it for so long, my lady. A combination of desperation, panic, and inexperience when it came to raising children. And now I'm ashamed to say that it's become something of a habit, but one that I have already decided to rectify as soon as possible."

"In the meantime, we're glad to have you here with us, Devon. And I think even the menacing Mrs. McCluddy will be hard pressed to make Finn and Heather unhappy when the Templeworth hoards descend."

"Can you imagine her trying to scold Lily or Ella?" Sophia asked with a grin. "Or George and Ollie, for that matter?"

"Even Nell would have the woman in tears," Cheska said proudly of their youngest niece.

"Of course she would," Adam said wryly. "She is of female Templeworth stock. Poor Mrs. McCluddy will be lucky to escape this Christmastide with her sanity."

They bantered back and forth for a bit, Adam declaring them the worst behaved ladies he'd ever encountered, which Sophia and Cheska laughingly objected to. In the end, they called a truce, declaring that whilst they *were* likely to be the worst behaved ladies in Christendom, they saw absolutely nothing wrong with that and therefore couldn't and wouldn't feel shame for it.

The duke, to his credit, merely looked a bit dazed by it all. Or as uncomfortable as Sophia often felt when the heat between Chesksa and Adam flared up and threatened to set them all on fire. Sophia was, unfortunately, well used to such things since she not only had to live with Cheska and Adam but also with Hope and Gideon, who were possibly worse, and Elle and Christian, who were just as bad even though Elodie was supposed to be the well-behaved one.

"Will you stay to dinner?" Cheska asked Sophia when she'd finished making mooneyes at her husband. "I know the others won't arrive for a few days, but it would be so nice to have you here with us this evening."

"Yes," Adam agreed with a sly grin. "If only to see you go toe to toe with the nanny again."

Sophia stuck her tongue out at him, which was extremely

childish, but she didn't care.

"I'd love to stay," she said with a sigh. "But Mama has invited Christian's aunt to dinner. *And* his cousin."

"The pig farmer?" Chesksa gasped, her horror mirroring Sophia's own reaction from earlier that day.

They both knew what it meant. They *all* knew what it meant. Philip Harrison had been in love with Elodie for years and when he'd lost her to his cousin, he'd turned his attentions to Hope who would have eaten him alive, Cheska who would have slapped him quicker than kiss him, and now apparently Sophia, who honestly didn't know *what* to do with him. He was one of the most boring, sweaty, boorish creatures she'd ever met. And she'd never forgiven him for how he'd almost ruined Elodie's happiness by spreading bitter, jealous rumors about her. Sophia had been a girl of twelve when that had happened, but that was no matter. She would never forgive anyone who hurt her sisters.

"That bloody man," Cheska spat in the most un-marchioness-like way possible. "He won't stop until he has you. Odious creature."

"I know. And Mama is beside herself with the idea of getting rid of me. I think she believes we somehow owe Philip a bride since Elodie ran off on him. And she must know that I have little chance or interest in getting her another lord for a son-in-law." Sophia had the vague notion that she should feel embarrassed discussing such personal things in front of a stranger. A duke, no less. But she couldn't bring herself to care. At least not about propriety. But it did suddenly occur to her just how pathetic she must seem to the handsome giant across from her, and humiliation churned in her gut at the idea that he should pity her.

Steeling herself to see that pity, or perhaps disgust, in his gaze, she risked a glance across the table. And the breath caught in her throat. For while she might not be able to name the dark emotion that she saw flashing in the depths of his eyes, she knew with certainty that it was about as far from pity or disgust as possible.

Chapter Four

D EVON FELT MORE than a little dazed as he sat back and listened to the Templeworth sisters talk about pig farmers and unwanted proposals. As a peer of the realm, he was used to ladies being quiet and demure around him. As a duke, he was more used to them being simpering and sycophantic.

Not so in the case of the marchioness and her willful, breeches-clad sister, clearly. He was torn between amusement, a kind of pity, and a bizarre sort of jealousy as Miss Templeworth explained her mother's machinations. And though he'd only been reacquainted with the chit for about an hour or so, as he sat admiring her vivacity, an outrageous idea was beginning to form in his head. One that he was quite sure was worthy of an extended stay in Bedlam. Yet, he could not shake it.

"Why not stay here then?" Lady Heywood offered once more. "If we send someone for your things, you won't even have to go back to explain yourself to Mama. She's not going to come and drag you home."

"Are you sure about that?" Miss Templeworth asked wryly.

"Well," the marchioness said with a devious grin, "she could try. But we both know that's never worked before."

"And Ares is here," Adam interjected wryly. "So, I know that if Cheska can't convince you to stay for *our* company, you'll most certainly stay for his."

Indeed, Miss Templeworth's eyes seemed to fairly glow at the mention of Adam's prized stallion.

"Well, yes. If I were going to pick who to spend my time with, it would be Ares," the lady laughed. "And it would be nice not to have Philip Harrison drooling at me over the venison."

"I'm flattered. Truly," the marchioness said dryly.

Devon kept his countenance, but that outrageous idea he'd just had grew and grew. Especially with talk of her staying here under the same roof as him.

He reflected on Heather's excited giggles, on Finn's shy smile…

"Miss Templeworth."

Three sets of eyes turned to face him as he spoke up.

"While I'm sure that Ares is as fine a beast as any Adam has ever possessed, you might be interested in my own mount, Aengus. I'd wager that there isn't a finer steed in England or Scotland. And he happens to be here with me."

He'd barely finished speaking when the chit was out of her chair and staring down at him. "Come on, then," she said. Demanded, more like.

"Oh—I, uh—now?" Devon was not used to feeling wrong-footed, but the tiny woman in breeches had him stuttering like a nervous school lad.

She frowned down at him. "Yes, now," she answered impatiently. "Are you otherwise engaged? Feeling exhausted from your journey?"

Devon didn't know whether to find her sarcasm insulting or endearing, but she didn't exactly give him a chance to decide, for she turned on her heels and marched from the room, leaving him to trail behind her trying not to notice the way those breeches fit her like a second skin. If Adam caught him salivating over his young sister-in-law, it would make for a deuced uncomfortable stay.

Keeping his eyes firmly above her waist, he followed her out to the stables, all the while that idea of his churning around in his mind. He would think it over, spend a couple of days deciding, watching her with Heather and Finn and trying to guess at her character. And then he'd decide if he were truly insane.

They reached the stables, and Devon watched as one by one the stable hands turned to gaze adoringly at Miss Templeworth. She greeted them all by name, not seeming to notice the blushes of the younger ones and veritable panting of the older. Or perhaps she did notice and just didn't care. *He* noticed. And though she was practically a stranger, he found that he cared. Just a little bit.

"Oh, my goodness."

Devon found himself slamming to a halt to avoid crashing into Sophia as she came to an abrupt stop. Right outside Aengus's stall.

"Oh, he's the most magnificent thing I've ever seen." The awe in her voice filled Devon with pride, and he stepped out from behind her so that he could peer down at her face. She turned her head to gaze up at him, and damned if he didn't feel the impact of those big, blue eyes right in his gut. "You must let me ride him."

Devon's heart stumbled a little. Not just from the way she was looking at him but in fear at the idea of her slight body on the huge beast. Aengus had been bred from warhorse stock. Not unlike Devon himself, his size harkened back to the days of fearsome Highland giants. The idea of the tiny bundle of energy bouncing on her toes before him on that colossal horse was enough to turn him gray.

"I don't think that's wise, Miss Templeworth. Aengus is incredibly strong. And he doesn't trust stra—"

He cut himself off and could only look in amazement as she rolled her eyes at him before closing the distance to Aengus and reached up to stroke his chestnut neck. Aengus, instead of whinnying grumpily and tossing his head, as he did with everyone except Devon and the stablemaster back at Farnshire, practically purred under the lady's ministrations.

"I do hope you're not implying that I wouldn't be able to handle this beauty. You might accidentally offend me." There was a dangerous glint in her eyes as they flashed at him. Hazardous enough that he was tempted to take a step back even though she barely came up to his chest.

"There are a great many men that cannot handle Aengus, Miss Templeworth."

Her smile was even more dangerous than that cobalt fire in her eyes. "I'm certain there are," she responded. "But I am no man."

It wasn't often that Devon Blake, Fourth Duke of Farnshire and descendant of Clan McFarn, found himself rendered speechless but here he was, shocked into silence by the tiny hoyden grinning up at him.

"But I—you..."

"I can see that understanding this information is going to take you a while, Your Grace. So why don't I just have Aengus here saddled up while you're working through it. By the time you've reached a conclusion, we'll be back safe and sound."

Devon could only watch, amazed into speechlessness, as the little termagant signaled for Aengus to be readied. The stable lad obviously took his silence for acquiescence. Or perhaps the young man knew better than to argue with Miss Templeworth. Either way, Devon stood there like a damned mute while she climbed atop his stallion, needing both the steps *and* the assistance of the stable boy to get up there.

Trepidation cracked through Devon's frozen surprise as he took in the sight of her on the giant horse. But she didn't give him the chance to voice his objections again as she threw him a cheeky grin before darting from the stables, her whoop of joy echoing in her wake. And it was only when she'd become a dot in the distance that he realized he'd been thoroughly insulted and bested by the incorrigible miss.

"DID MY MOTHER threaten to come and drag me home kicking and screaming, Bessie?"

Bessie, who had been Sophia's abigail and friend since her Come Out merely smiled at Sophia's outrageous question. "She caught me slipping out the back, Miss. But I was able to get away fairly quickly." It had been the height of cowardice, Sophia knew, to send a note to Bessie instructing the maid to pack up her things and travel to Heywood Manor with them. But the truth was that she simply didn't have the energy for a showdown with Mama about Philip the pig farmer. And besides, she'd used up all her bravery when she'd confiscated Lord Farnshire's horse.

Even now, after an hour soaking in a lavender bath, her muscles still stretched painfully when she moved. She, who had spent almost her entire life on horses. Who had stolen marvelous steeds from Christian, Gideon, *and* Adam and had managed them all with ease. But Aengus—Aengus was a different breed altogether. And for the first time in her life, Sophia had felt a twinge of trepidation as she'd galloped across Adam's grounds, even as exhilaration thrummed through her veins.

The duke, she'd realized, had been right to warn her to be careful with Aengus. And in her usual fashion, she'd chosen not to listen. But as she'd cleared the hedge that bordered Adam's formal gardens, the thrill of the ride took over, and her fears had slipped away with every hoof beat upon the frozen ground. Now, however, she was feeling the effects. Her legs, her buttocks, even her *arms* were sore.

Still, it had been worth it to see the look of shock on that devilishly handsome face of his. Sophia never tired of proving naysayers wrong about her. Men who thought her incapable because of her size or sex. Women who thought her odd and undesirable because she wore breeches and avoided men like the plague.

She had delighted in besting the duke. Moreso than any other man of her acquaintance. He overset her in a way that was both unfamiliar and vastly annoying. But as much as she might be delighted about it, she was still bloody sore!

"Here we are, Miss." Bessie stood at the edge of the tub holding out the linens that she'd been warming by the fire. Outside, a snow that had been threatening all day began to fall in soft, fat flakes, and Sophia was never more grateful that her sisters had managed to get wealthy lords to fall in love with them. If they'd married paupers, they'd all be freezing in the harsh conditions. As it was, Adam kept Heywood Manor delightfully warm.

Groaning at the tightness in her muscles, she stood and slowly, carefully climbed from the tub. She didn't usually have Bessie help her out of the bathtub like an infant. And she always kept her ablutions to a minimum with as little preening as she could get away with. But this evening she needed all the help she could get.

Sitting at the dressing table in an unusual act of biddability, Sophia caught Bessie's poor attempt at hiding her smile. "I'm glad my agony amuses you so," she said dryly to the maid who promptly burst into a fit of giggles, her wild curls bouncing with the action.

"I'm sorry, Miss. But I haven't seen you so sore in years. The duke's beast certainly seemed to put you to work."

"Indeed, he did," Sophia groused, but she couldn't keep a grin of exhilaration from her face as she remembered the thrill of riding such a magnificent creature. "Though I cannot deny I'm already excited to have at him again."

"Not for a while yet, I hope," Bessie said as she pinned Sophia's hair atop her head. Sophia didn't know how Bessie managed to tame her hair into something sophisticated and didn't usually care one way or another. Yet tonight she found that she wanted to look her best. Or at least look remotely put together. And she didn't care to examine too closely why that was.

"I might need to give my backside a chance to recover," Sophia answered baldly. She'd never been one to mince her words and certainly not with those close to her. "But it hopefully won't take too long. He's a beauty, Bessie."

"The horse or the duke, Miss?"

Sophia spun around on her stool to stare up at the maid, hating the heat she could feel seeping into her cheeks.

"What do you mean?" she demanded.

"Oh, nothing. It's just that there's no denying he's a handsome man. And, well, he's single. You're single. And you'll be spending all this time around each other. I just thought—"

"There's nothing to think," Sophia said a little sharply. She hated how defensive she sounded. Hated how odd Bessie's comments and innuendos made her feel. Would the duke think that she'd somehow contrived to stay here just to be around him? To ensnare him? She knew that such things were embarrassingly commonplace among the Quality. Her mother's own machinations were proof enough of that. But Sophia would never lower herself to try to trap a man, no matter how handsome or wealthy he was, no matter how powerful his title.

She'd have to disabuse him of that notion—if indeed he had such a notion.

"I meant no harm, Miss." Bessie's contrite words made Sophia feel immediately ashamed of her snappy tone. She never got annoyed with Bessie. She just felt so *unsettled* this evening.

"I'm sorry, Bessie," she said as she stood and shook out her ice-blue skirts. "I don't know what is wrong with me today."

Bessie waved off her apologies and handed over a white shawl in difference to the drafts that ran through the corridors of the house. "Perhaps it's just one of those days, Miss. Enjoy your evening."

Sophia smiled and hurried from the room, but as she rushed toward the dining room, she couldn't help but think there'd been an annoyingly knowing look on the maid's face as she'd bid her goodnight.

Chapter Five

" AH, THERE YOU are. Late as usual."

Sophia stuck her tongue out at Francesca as she glided into the room. Yes, she was late. And yes, it was usual for her to be late. But one would think that they should all be well used to it by now.

Besides, the blasted stairs had taken an age on account of her stiffness. Not that she'd ever admit such a thing. She batted away Cheska's attempt at a shove before casting her eyes about the room.

Adam was conversing with the duke, who looked darkly intimidating in a charcoal jacket and tight, black breeches. They both looked her way, Adam rolling his eyes at her and Cheska's squabbling, and the duke seeming irritatingly smug as he ran a discerning gaze over her.

"Why are you walking so funnily?" Francesca asked, and the duke's sudden grin was answer enough that he *was* feeling smug, no doubt guessing at the toll his warhorse had taken on her body.

"I'm not walking funnily," she grumbled.

It was to be just the four of them this evening, she knew, with the hordes not due to descend for some time yet. So, there would be no avoiding him and that stupid, knowing look on his handsome face.

"Did you enjoy your ride with Aengus, lass—er, Miss Sophia?" the duke asked, his tone vaguely mocking, and Sophia was surprised by the little thrill that went through her at his slip up in calling her "lass." She didn't know if it was the odd intimacy of the word itself or the almost imperceptible Scottish brogue, but it did funny things to her insides, and she did *not* appreciate this giant, arrogant brute having any effect on her insides whatsoever.

"Oh, it was marvelous, Your Grace," she said airily. "He's such a placid, docile thing. I confess, I'm surprised you find him so difficult to manage." She bit her lip to contain her laugher at the look of utter shock on his face. A look which quickly turned into a scowl of displeasure.

"I don't find him difficult to manage, Miss Templeworth," he ground out between clenched teeth. "I was just worried that the ride might have taken its toll on a delicate miss such as yourself."

It was Sophia's turn to scowl as her temper flared. And it didn't help that Francesca snorted, and Adam made a poor attempt at covering up his laugh after the duke's comment. He was a conceited oaf, implying that she was some delicate little girl who couldn't handle his horse when he knew perfectly well, had seen with his own eyes in fact, that she could.

She was tempted to smack that face of his. More tempted to tell him exactly what she thought of him. But Francesca knew her well and stepped in front of her before she had a chance to open her mouth.

"Is that a new gown, Sophia? It's darling on you."

"Yes," she snapped. "Your Grace if you think that I'm—"

"Uncle Devon."

They turned as one at the sound of a timid voice in the doorway, to see the duke's nephew hovering there, his dark eyes huge in his face. He was a handsome little thing, Sophia noted, he looked just like his uncle. Hopefully, he hadn't inherited any of the man's characteristics.

"Finn, lad. What are you doing down here by yourself?"

The boy's gaze darted from the duke, to Sophia, then to Cheska and Adam before landing back on his uncle.

"I-I couldn't sleep," he answered uncertainly, and Sophia's

heart went out to the mite. He looked so afraid, so sad. It was heartbreaking.

"Where is Mrs. McCluddy?" the duke frowned, and though Sophia could see that it wasn't with displeasure or unkindness, she also saw the lad flinch infinitesimally. She wished that the duke would get down to the boy's level, open his arms to him, make sure he knew it was fine for him to be here. It was clear that the child could use the reassurance.

"Sh-she's asleep, Uncle Devon. She always falls asleep after her wee dram. And she said we mustn't wake her. But I was scared a-and I didn't know what else to do."

"What's a wee dram?" Francesca whispered loudly enough to wake the dead.

"I have no idea," Sophia mumbled back.

The duke's sigh sounded like it came from the depths of his soul, and Sophia was shocked by the sympathy that coursed through her when only moments ago she'd been wanting to do him bodily harm.

"It's whiskey. And by the sounds of it, a lot of it," Adam muttered, his voice laced with fury.

"That bloody woman," Sophia exclaimed. And then before the duke could answer, before she even thought about what she was doing, she was kneeling in front of Finn just as she'd done with his sister earlier, her skirts once again paying the price.

"Hello, Finn. Do you remember me? I'm Sophia."

The little boy's eyes widened, but he nodded, the candle in his hand shaking slightly.

"It can be a little frightening staying somewhere new, can't it?" she continued in a voice she usually reserved for particularly skittish horses that she broke in. "You know, I'm only visiting here, too. My house is on the other side of the village."

"It is?"

"Indeed. Quite a way away. But you know what always helps me to sleep here even though it's not my own bedchamber?"

"What?"

Sophia hid her smile at the boy's breathless interest, striving to keep her face solemn.

"A magic drink that only Lady Heywood's cook knows how to make," she whispered, leaning in and hiding her smile once more as he leaned in, too.

"Magic?" he repeated in awe.

"Magic," she said with faux seriousness. "But it's a very powerful recipe, and so it's a secret, so we mustn't let the others know about it. If I take you to Cook, do you think it might work on you?"

"Yes," Finn answered, his nerves seeming to be quite forgotten. "I'm sure it will, and I promise, I shan't tell anyone. Not even Heather."

"Well then, let's see if we can convince Cook to prepare some so that you can sleep soundly until you get used to your new quarters, shall we?"

She stood back up and held a hand out to the little boy who hesitated only fleetingly before grasping it. Her heart ached as he gazed up at her with those shy but thankfully trusting eyes.

Turning her head to take in the other three occupants gazing at them, she shrugged. "It looks like I'll be late to dinner," she said before gently pulling the boy from the room with her. She realized as they hurried along the well-lit corridor toward the kitchens, that she'd once again rather put herself in the middle of where she didn't belong. She had commandeered the duke's nephew without even speaking to the man.

It was just as the youngest of four sisters, the oldest of whom had always been as close to perfect as a woman could get, the other two with personalities large enough take over every room they entered, sometimes it hadn't been easy putting herself forward or speaking up for what she wanted. Yes, she'd cured herself of that particular issue before she'd been in long skirts, but it hadn't always been easy to be heard. And she had a feeling that little Finn felt the same way.

There was nothing in the duke's demeanor to suggest that he

was unkind to the children or that he didn't care about them. And he might be an arrogant cad to her, but he wasn't cruel. Adam wouldn't be friends with him if he were. Besides, she'd known from their first meeting last year that he was fundamentally good. When they'd shared that one dance, when he'd held her as though she were made of glass...

"Ouch!"

"Are you well, M-miss?"

Sophia rubbed at her head. Foolish wool-gathering about the duke and the dancing and what happened? She'd walked into the banisters of the stairs.

"Just stumbled a little," she reassured the boy airily. "Why don't you call me Sophia?" she continued as they began the descent to the kitchens. Francesca's staff were so used to Sophia now that she came and went as much as she pleased, so it wouldn't be a surprise to have her show up at this hour. At least she hoped not. She knew that Cook had been in something of a tizzy about having to feed a duke for weeks, and she didn't want to add anything to the woman's workload.

But the little one was distressed. And if a cup of warm milk helped him settle down, then she'd risk the woman's ire.

"Uncle Devon said it's not gentlemanly to address a lady informally," Finn said solemnly.

"Ah. Well, His Grace is right, I suppose. But then again, we are friends. Or at least I hope we are. And I think that it's quite proper for friends to call each other by their names. So I shall be Sophia, and you shall be Finn. How does that sound?"

"That sounds wonderful, Sophia." His smile was so much easier this time, and Sophia's heart clenched at the sight.

"Here we are," she said past the odd tightening in her throat. "Mrs. Leighton, I'm sorry to disturb you at such a busy time, but I wondered if you'd be able to make Master Finn some of that secret, magical milk that helps me sleep when I'm here."

Thankfully, Finn was so busy looking around the bustling kitchen that he didn't notice Sophia's less-than-subtle wink in the cook's direction.

"Ah—y-yes, of course, Miss. It won't take me a moment to rustle some up. But..." The cook darted a glance around the kitchen where a veritable army of servants were looking flustered as they busily put together dish after dish, and Sophia could see that they were in the way.

"Why don't we go back upstairs and wait for you to find the—ah—magic powder that you use? I know you keep it somewhere very secret and safe."

Once again, Mrs. Leighton caught on to the scheme immediately, and she nodded with some relief. "Of course, Miss Templeworth. Shall I send the boy's drink to the nursery?"

Sophia looked down into Finn's face and saw the worry once again present in his eyes. He didn't want to be left alone in the nursery with only his baby sister and an old drunkard for company. Neither of whom would be awake with him. She knew how it felt to be left alone, to be lonely.

"No, we shall go and join the others," Sophia declared, though she well knew that children absolutely did not attend adult dinner parties. But she didn't care. When the family were together, they dined casually. And while it was true that her nieces and nephews were always well asleep before the adults sat down to dinner, it was also true that if one of them needed their parents or even their aunt, they wouldn't be sent away alone and afraid.

Taking Finn's hand once more, she hurried them back to the drawing room, chattering away as they went, telling Finn all about her horses and listening as he told her about the pony his Uncle Devon had purchased on his last birthday.

They neared the drawing room, and Sophia began to feel a little trepidation. She didn't know the duke well enough to know what he might make of her antics with his nephew. Some peers, she knew, were absolute sticklers for rules, and a duke probably more so given the weight of such a title.

Perhaps he would be angry, berate her for teaching his nephew bad manners and for interfering where she very much didn't belong.

Well, she told herself as she squared her shoulders, she wouldn't be sorry for helping the mite even if it gained her the ill-favor of a duke. She would simply have to bear his displeasure and deal with his disapproval.

Steeling herself for both, Sophia pushed open the door and walked in with Finn's hand firmly in her grasp. Francesca smiled and waved. Adam and Lord Farnshire both jumped to their feet, and while she looked briefly at Adam, her gaze was drawn to the duke. Her heart stopped, then burst into a gallop as her eyes met his. And while she had expected anger, perhaps disgust, she couldn't have imagined that he would look at her with something like tenderness in depths of his own.

Chapter Six

D EVON FOUND HIMSELF not knowing quite what to feel as he took in the picture before him. Only minutes ago, he'd been debating whether he wanted to seduce Sophia Templeworth or antagonize her some more. He wasn't used to people being anything other than scraping and groveling around him. He certainly wasn't used to a slip of a thing implying that he couldn't handle his own damned horse.

Yet, coupled with the vague irritation, there'd been a decidedly potent lust coursing through him. Perhaps he was a glutton for punishment, but that smart mouth of hers was doing treacherous things to his libido, he had to admit.

She was just so amusing. That was it. He didn't find himself amused by much these days, and certainly not by the vapid ladies of Quality he usually encountered. But this Miss Templeworth, she was a different matter altogether. He'd suspected it last year. He knew it without a doubt now. She would absolutely drive him insane. But she'd keep him entertained and on his toes. Even her stubbornly refusing to admit that she'd found Aengus trying was amusing to him, especially when anyone with eyes could see that she was hobbling and wincing as she went.

He'd been quite looking forward to provoking her some more over the roast beef, if only to see what shocking retort she'd come up with, when Finn had come into the drawing room shivering and looking like a lost lamb. All trace of amusement had disappeared at the sight of the boy and his lone candle, staring at them all as though he'd seen a ghost.

And damn him, but Devon hadn't known what to do. He hated that he felt so uncomfortable around the lad. Hated that he didn't know how to comfort him, how to make everything better for him and for Heather. But he was as useless now as he had been when the guardianship first started.

So while he stood there like an idiot, frozen and unsure, Sophia Templeworth once again shocked him to his core by taking charge. He could only watch, torn between gratitude and an odd sort of tenderness as she dropped in front of Finn and spoke to him in a soft, coaxing voice. She spoke of magic and all sorts of nonsense, but it was working. He watched in amazement as Finn's trembling stopped, as he reached out and took her hand and disappeared with her as though in her thrall. And Devon knew the feeling! He felt rather in her thrall himself.

In the silence left in their wake, he'd turned to Adam and Lady Heywood, but neither of them had seemed remotely surprised by the girl's behavior, by the fact that she'd popped herself onto the floor in a gown that must have cost a tidy sum, or that she'd been rabbiting on about magical drinks, or even that she'd just swept from the room, Finn in hand, unbothered by the fact that they were due to dine in only minutes.

And he'd just stood there, not knowing if he should rush after his nephew or leave him with the slightly deranged but undeniably kind Sophia Templeworth. Stood there while that idea of his, the one he hadn't been able to get out of his mind since he'd seen her again this afternoon, had bounced around incessantly in his head.

And now, here she was again. Finn grinning broadly by her side. And the tenderness that swept through Devon in that moment was enough to wash away every thought of annoyance or irritation or wounded pride.

"Mrs. Leighton is taking care of something special for Finn and me, so we're just going to wait here until it's done," Sophia said, her chin tilted defiantly as though she expected some sort of argument from him.

Did she think he would object, Devon wondered, trying not to be stung by the idea. Did she think he was some sort of tyrant that would send a scared little boy off by himself? And just like that, as quickly as the annoyance had dispersed it was back again with a bang. But he didn't snap at her. For one thing, he didn't want Finn being afraid again. He looked far more at ease with Sophia Templeworth than he ever did with him. He *wanted* the lad here. He wanted to know that Finn was well. That he would perhaps sleep easily tonight. If Sophia Templeworth and her bossiness and nonsensical talk could make that happen, Devon was all for it.

"Sophia said I could wait in here, Uncle Devon," Finn said, and Devon hated that the hesitancy was in the boy's voice once more. Why was Finn so scared of him? He didn't shout. He wasn't a brute.

"I told him it was fine for us to use our given names, since we're friends. I do hope that isn't a problem, Your Grace?"

Devon looked from Finn to Sophia Templeworth and back again. It seemed that they both thought he was going to haul them over the coals for this. And while he didn't particularly like that the chit had overstepped, *again,* he also wasn't so boorish as to make a fuss of it. Frankly, he didn't feel as though he deserved Finn's nervousness or Sophia's obstinance.

"No problem at all, Miss Templeworth," he said, raising a brow at the challenge in her face. "Perhaps if I'm lucky, I, too, will manage to gain your friendship in time and disperse with formalities."

He watched with no small amount of amusement and a healthy dose of desire as a soft blush made its way across her cheeks. She might be willful and adversarial, but she wasn't immune to some light flirtation, which pleased him to no end. Probably more than it should.

Adam's less-than-subtle cough was a timely reminder, however, that they were not alone, and he should probably watch what he said in front of an overprotective brother-in-law who was a crack shot.

Before he could explain himself or get shot, the door opened again, and there was Adam's butler, Severin, a silver tray in hand. "Your—er—magic drink, Miss Templeworth," the older man said. "And my lord, my lady, dinner is served."

"Thank you, Severin," Lady Heywood smiled at the butler, and damned if the old codger didn't blush a little. Devon was quite pleased to see that even the most stoic of creatures wasn't immune to the charms of the Templeworth ladies.

"Come along then, Finn, lad. Let's say goodnight and get you back to the nursery." He held his hand out to Finn, his heart sinking when the boy held tight to Sophia. He tried not to flinch at the action, but it felt like a punch to the gut.

"I want Sophia to take me, Uncle Devon," Finn said in that timid voice that made Devon feel like a monster. He hated that he made Finn feel discomfited. He hated that Adam and his wife and Sophia Templeworth were privy to this humiliating exchange. But for the sake of Finn's feelings, and his own pride, he pasted a smile on his face.

"Of course," he said, hoping that he sounded more jovial than he felt. "I can…"

"How about," the interfering miss piped up to interrupt him. But she was looking at him now, not combatively, but with something like kindness and not pity, but sympathy perhaps. "How about we ask Uncle Devon to escort us so that I can carry the tray and he can make sure we get there safely in the dark. Especially after our little incident on the way to the kitchen," she said with a wink, earning herself a giggle from Finn. A *giggle*. Devon realized, his heart twisting, that he'd never heard the boy laugh.

And Devon could have dropped to his knees in gratitude. Not only because she'd elicited a laugh from his solemn nephew, but because she'd clearly somehow sensed his desire to care for the boy and had found a way to bring him a step closer to that.

"Maybe Uncle Devon can hold the candle for us," Finn said, and Devon was floored by how such a simple thing could make him feel ten feet tall.

"An excellent idea, Finn," Sophia said brightly, dropping the boy's hand and plucking the tray from the butler's. "If Your Grace will lead us, we shall be on our way. We don't want the magic to wear out, after all."

"Miss Templeworth, the dinner…"

"Don't bother, Severin," Lady Heywood interrupted the bemused servant. "Sophia wouldn't care if we all starved. His lordship and I will come directly. His Grace and my tearaway sister will follow when they've escorted Master Finn to the nursery."

"Jolly good," Sophia said stoutly, not seeming to care in the slightest that her sister had casually labeled her a tearaway. Just as the marchioness didn't seem to care that she was speaking in such a manner about her sister, and to a servant.

Devon looked to Adam for his reaction, but he didn't react to the interchange, obviously used to it and unbothered by it. Devon found it quite liberating to be around ladies who didn't act as though personalities of any kind were things to be buried in satins and stiff upper lips. And so, when she marched from the room and Finn grinned broadly, handing Devon his candle, and rushing out after her, Devon found himself grinning right along with his nephew.

SOPHIA'S HEART WAS hammering at a rather alarming pace as she stood back and allowed the duke to walk ahead of her, with Finn as a sort of buffer between them. She had caught Cheska's knowing grin as she'd taken the tray from Severin, but she was choosing to ignore it, just as she was choosing to ignore that stupid fluttering in her stomach that had started when the duke had looked so crestfallen at Finn's rejection.

She knew that she was being incredibly overbearing. Some of it because her heart ached for the children, some of it because the duke made her feel wrongfooted every time she was around him, and she was trying to brazen it out. But then he'd looked so grateful for her intervention, so pleased that she'd included him in this madcap little adventure and, well, the stomach fluttering and heart hammering had been rampant ever since.

Finn, who had apparently found his tongue, peppered her with questions about the rapidly cooling milk she was now carrying on a silver tray, and she was forced to talk complete gibberish to explain away the cinnamon that she could smell in it. She was more thankful than she could say that Mrs. Leighton had played along, but she did rather wish she'd found a way to ask the cook what she planned on putting into the drink.

Still, she seemed to be holding her own with Finn believing her, and she was delighted when Lord Farnshire took up the thread and began to tell Finn of a legend surrounding a witch in Farnshire who'd made potions and cast spells for the locals, including Finn's own great-great-grandfather. Sophia found herself listening avidly to the tale, though she knew it was a silly faery story. But there was something so mesmerizing about the duke's deep voice, the mellifluous lilt, the hint of a Scottish brogue.

She almost walked into a wooden post again.

They finally reached the nursery, and sure enough, when the duke pushed the door open, Sophia could tell just from the stiffness in his broad shoulders that he wasn't happy with what he saw. Finn pushed by him into the room, and then because she was far too curious to wait, Sophia pushed past him, too. The room was filled with toys, with a darling little dining table and four wooden chairs in the middle. Francesca had decorated the nursery before she'd even been *enceinte* due to their nieces and nephews and their frequent visits, so it was well-equipped to house Heather and Finn. But the duke's dark glare was not aimed at the playroom. Nay, he was glaring at the door to Mrs. McCluddy's bedchamber. The door which was fully opened to reveal Mrs. McCluddy sprawled face down on the bed, a bottle of what Sophia assumed was the infamous whiskey still clutched in her hand.

The woman's snores were loud enough to wake the dead, and Sophia hurried forward to shut her door, salvaging a tiny bit of the old dragon's pride, and saving their ears from the noise. Once the door had shut with a firm click, she turned back to see Finn staring wide-eyed toward the bedchamber, and the duke towering above him looking as though he could happily tear something apart with his bare hands. She marveled briefly at the picture they painted, their matching sable hair and dark-as-night eyes. But she could see that Finn was growing concerned again, and that the duke was once again looking utterly lost, so she pasted a smile on her face, handing the duke the tray and plucking the cup of milk from it.

"Come along then, Finn," she said, keeping her voice to a whisper. The door to the children's bedchamber was open a crack, too, and she pushed it further to see little Heather fast asleep, thumb in mouth and looking positively angelic with her mop of raven curls framing her face.

"It's very important that you're already tucked up in bed when you drink this," she whispered to Finn, and he dutifully scrambled under the covers. "It's very potent, so it gets to work almost right away. Now, here you go." She handed him the cup of now-tepid milk and watched with a grin as he eagerly downed the contents. He handed her the empty cup and lay back against the pillows, his eyes widening as they moved from Sophia to the duke, who now stood in the doorway, and back again.

"I think it's working," he whispered back in awe, and his innocence melted Sophia's heart.

"Well, it's very strong magic," she said, all seriousness. Then, because she couldn't help it, she leaned down and pressed a kiss against the boy's head. "Close your eyes," she instructed softly. He immediately did so. "And think hard about what you'd like to dream of."

Finn cracked open one eye. "What do you like to dream of?" he asked.

"Usually my horses," Sophia answered, a little embarrassed knowing that the duke could hear. It felt—intimate—to be whispering of her dreams in his hearing. But she was only settling the child, she assured herself, not revealing the secrets of her soul. "Sometimes I dream of being a pirate queen and going on grand adventures over the seas."

"Oh, I like that one," Finn declared. "I shall be a pirate, too. Only—I shall be a *king*."

"An excellent choice," she laughed. "Now, go ahead and start dreaming. And you can tell me all about it tomorrow."

"Goodnight, Sophia," he said. "Goodnight, Uncle Devon."

Sophia looked over at the duke, whose eyes looked suspiciously bright in the flickering candlelight. "Goodnight, lad," the duke said gruffly. "Sleep well."

They both tiptoed from the room, not wanting to disturb Heather. When Lord Farnshire hesitated outside Mrs. McCluddy's door, Sophia acted on instinct, reaching out to grab hold of his arm and pull him into the darkened corridor outside. Or at least, he allowed himself to be pulled. Judging from the size of the muscle under her fingers, he would find it laughably easy to set her aside. But he allowed it. And when they got outside the room, she turned to look up at him, not quite knowing what to say. And not knowing why she couldn't seem to want to remove her hand from his arm.

Chapter Seven

D EVON STOOD IN the darkened hallway, trying to understand his body's reaction to the simplest of touches from Sophia Templeworth. He felt as though he were being tossed around in a maelstrom of feelings that he didn't know how to handle.

He was livid with that damned McCluddy woman. Livid with his mother for insisting on keeping her on. But more than anything, he was upset with himself for leaving the children in her charge for so long.

Looking down into the delicately lovely face of Sophia Templeworth, he knew that that idea of his from earlier was a lot less madcap than he'd been telling himself. Of course, it was still far too early to be thinking such things. And he wasn't convinced that Adam would let him live afterward. But there was no denying that her situation and his would benefit from what he was thinking.

Namely, a marriage.

An insane thought on the surface, but there was merit to it.

She was inching toward spinsterhood, and if her reaction to the pig farmer was anything to go by, she had no intentions of avoiding that state for just anybody. But he was a duke. She would be a duchess. That wasn't to be sniffed at. And while she seemed fiercely independent, he knew that she was the single daughter of a widowed, untitled lady. From his correspondence with Adam over the past year, he knew that Mr. Templeworth hadn't cared a whit for his daughters and wouldn't have made provisions for them.

Sophia Templeworth was a proud woman. She wouldn't like relying on the kindness of her sisters to fund her life. Not forever. Her beauty would be enough to land her a husband, but he'd have to contend with that viper's tongue of hers, and he didn't think anyone around here would be up for that particular challenge. Besides, she didn't belong in a small town with a pig farmer. She was meant for more. And he could see her in Farnshire, and at all his other seats. He could imagine her riding over the lands, taking the children on adventures, talking about magic and witches, even managing to get *him* talking about such things, and filling his sometimes desolate houses with fun and laughter.

Her relationship with Adam meant that he couldn't offer her a position as a governess. She was too well-connected to be hired help, and he valued his friendship with Adam too much to turn the man's sister-in-law into a servant.

And as an added bonus, to make the idea perhaps less shocking and more appealing, he was thinking with his head and not the other, more demanding parts of his anatomy. Even if he did find the chit uncommonly attractive. This wasn't about that. She was good with the children; he'd seen that even in their brief interactions. She was a lot more fun, and while his mother would probably be appalled by her forthrightness and would worry about her passing it on to the children, he could only think that Finn would benefit from her bold demeanor. He couldn't imagine a man alive who would be able to take advantage of her, so if some of that rubbed off on Heather? Well, that could only be a good thing.

Someone in his position needed to make logical, sensible decisions about such things. As a duke and the guardian of two grieving children, he couldn't afford to let silly things like feelings get in the way of doing what would benefit the children most. Which was exactly why he should offer for Miss Templeworth now, marry her, and take her back to Farnshire with him so she could help him navigate the tough waters of parenthood.

Yes, there really was no downside that he could think of. She was a clever woman. Bright, intelligent, if a little loudmouthed. She would see the merit in such a plan.

"Your Grace? Are you well? I know that you must be angry about that cranky old goat, but you look fit to be tied and, frankly, it wouldn't be a good idea to throw a tantrum and wake the children."

Her words were like a slap to the face. A tantrum! He had never been accused of throwing a tantrum in his life. Not even as a boy. She was maddening. Utterly, infuriatingly maddening. Here he'd been thinking of offering her a title, as a *duchess* for God's sake. And she was accusing him of throwing tantrums.

Just like that, all thoughts of logic and sense simply flew away. How could he have been thinking of offering for her? She would be a nightmare. He'd thought her candor would be a good thing for the children, and perhaps it would be, but it wouldn't make up for the headache he would be bound to have around her.

"I was *not* throwing a tantrum. While I'm furious with Mrs. McCluddy, I know better than to cause a scene with my niece and nephew not ten feet away, I'll have you know."

"Fine." She dropped her hand from his arm, and he felt even more annoyed with her because he missed it and that was ridiculous. "But you were looking so serious, and I know that I want to throw the woman out a window for being in such a state around the children, so I imagined you were feeling the same way."

"I do have some self-control, Miss Templeworth. You are the one standing here talking about throwing people out of a window."

"I'm sure you do, Your Grace," she snorted, rolling her eyes, her tone dripping with sarcasm. "Of course, a big, important duke knows how to contain himself and behave himself at all times.

Never stepping out of line. Never crossing boundaries. Am I right?"

Her words snapped the last, tiny vestiges of his control. Since he'd arrived this morning, since meeting her last year, in fact, she'd been driving him mad. Whether he found her infuriating or endearing, baffling or alluring, he hadn't stopped thinking about her.

The idea of her finding him staid or boring, only ever doing what was right, only ever caring about what was proper made his already tenuous grip on himself dissolve completely. And before he could even attempt to get hold of it again, the candle he was holding fell to the ground, plunging them into even more darkness, and then his hands were reaching out as if of their own volition, pulling her flush against him.

"No," he growled, "You are *not* right," he said before bending his head and capturing her mouth in a searing kiss.

SOPHIA HAD A moment—just one moment—of complete and utter shock before her body lit up in flames. She'd never experienced anything like the desperate, heated yearning rushing through her. Some small part of her brain wondered at his actions—and her own. That same small part tried to stop her from wrapping her arms around his neck, from standing on her toes to press herself closer to his rock-hard body. But it was useless. She succumbed to him entirely and enthusiastically.

She'd never felt anything like the emotions coursing through her veins in that moment. Her limbs felt as though they were made of liquid fire, and she could do nothing but cling to the duke and surrender to his expert ministrations. The feel of his mouth pressed against her own was exquisite, but it awakened within her something wicked, something dark, and when his tongue ran along the seam of her lips before delving inside her mouth, she could only think that she wanted more and more and more.

Guided purely by instinct, she mirrored his actions and was rewarded with a tortured groan, and the hand that had been wrapped around her waist was suddenly on the move, delving into her hair, tugging her head back, wrapping around the loosened strands. She had to stop this. She needed to stop. But then she was moving. With a muffled oath, the duke turned her and pressed her against the wall, pressing himself closer until he was all she could feel and smell and taste.

Sophia was an innocent, but not entirely naïve. Who could be, with Hope Templeworth as a sister? So she knew exactly what the hardness pressed against her meant. Just as she knew that the torturous hunger inside her could only be sated by this man.

The hands that had gripped her hair just moments ago were on the move again, this time tracing her curves until he'd wrung a moan from the depths of her soul, then moving to her skirts and pulling them up. Her breathing was embarrassingly loud in the stillness of the night, but she couldn't bring herself to care. Not when her entire being was engulfed in flames.

"Please," she begged. She who had never been reduced to begging a man for anything in her life. She didn't even know what it was she was asking for. Just that she wanted more of what he was doing. Just that somehow, only he could give her what she needed.

He pulled his lips from hers only to trail kisses along her jaw, to bite gently against the skin of her neck. "I know, lass," the duke whispered against her throat, his breathing as labored as her own. "Christ, I need to get a hold of myself," he groaned, sounding as though he were in the worst sort of pain.

"Frankly, I'd rather you kept hold of me," Sophia answered bluntly, if a little desperately.

His breathless laugh against her skin sent a shiver of pleasure skittering along her spine, and that aching need inside of her grew unbearable.

"I—"

"Sophia, where have you gotten to? It can't take—oh."

The sound of Cheska's voice rent the air and had Lord Farnshire springing back away from Sophia as though she'd burned him. Odd, since it suddenly felt as though she'd been doused in ice water. "Sophia. What on earth are doing? Put that man down before—"

"What in the hell are you doing? Get off her, you bastard."

Francesca sighed. "Before Adam sees you."

It was only then that Sophia realized she was still clinging to the duke, her arms still wrapped around him even though he'd moved away from crushing her against the wall.

"Adam, I can explain," Sophia said, snatching her hands back.

"Oh, can you?" he drawled sarcastically. "I can't wait to hear it."

"Sweetheart, calm down. You don't even know what happened."

"Calm down?" Adam yelled, his head whipping around to Francesca. "Calm *down*? I let him stay here. I *trusted* him. And the second my back is turned, he's manhandling your sister."

"In his defense, it looked like mutual handling to me," Cheska said, totally unperturbed by Adam's ire.

Sophia nodded her agreement. She was beyond mortified to have been found like this. But she couldn't allow Adam to think that the duke had accosted her and attacked her. Firstly, because it wasn't fair, and secondly because she found it rather insulting that he would think her incapable of a good accosting.

"Francesca, my love. You are not helping," Adam said through gritted teeth.

"Helping with what?" she shrugged. "Sophia looks just fine. Mussed, but fine. So, no harm done. And unless you think that your friend, who has *been* your friend through ups and downs and thick and thin, is the type to take advantage of my sister while she was fighting him off, then I'd say you don't know him very well." Francesca paused before raising a brow at Sophia. "Or her, for that matter."

"Sweetheart, you know I don't give a damn about rules and propriety. But I have to face Christian and Gideon in a few days. And even if I didn't care about them thinking I couldn't protect Sophia, you must know that there are some things that I simply cannot allow to happen under my roof. Your sister is an innocent. A lady of Quality. If I don't—"

"I'm standing right here, Adam," Sophia snapped. She could feel the heat scalding her cheeks, so she knew her face must be positively scarlet. And it was hard enough trying to get her muddled thoughts in order after what had just happened between her and the duke without having her overbearing brother-in-law talk about her as though she wasn't there.

"Oh, I bloody well know you are," Adam shot back, but the glint of fury in his eyes was trained very much on the duke. Sophia had the sudden mad urge to throw herself into his arms. Whether to protect herself or him she didn't quite know. "And you," her furious brother-in-law continued, turning fully to glare at the duke. "You think that you can waltz into my home, accept my hospitality, and then what? Seduce my damned sister right under my nose?"

"It's not what you think."

Sophia, who had opened her mouth to argue with Adam, closed it again and turned to stare at the duke. Not what he thought? Much as she would like this embarrassing spectacle to be glossed over, even she knew that it was obvious what they'd been doing. When Elodie and Christian had been found in a compromising situation years ago, it had been a genuine series of unfortunate events. Because Elodie was pure and good. Sophia was not. And this was no misunderstanding. In fact, she couldn't even say what would have happened if Cheska hadn't caught them moments ago. But judging by the anger on Adam's face, it would have been enough to make the marquess's head explode.

Adam's laugh held not a trace of amusement, and Sophia darted a look at her sister, who simply rolled her eyes. "I think it's exactly what I think," Adam said, and even though the sentence was a little convoluted, it still managed to sound threatening. "Are you really going to deny that you've just been pawing at her like a damned animal, Devon? What, you thought a little seduction to pass the time while you're here and then you'll run off back to Scotland and leave us here cleaning up your mess?"

Sophia's temper ignited at Adam's words. In a roundabout way she knew he was being protective but calling her a mess was beyond the pale!

She opened her mouth to tell him just that, but the duke got there first.

"No, you damned idiot," he bit out sounding every bit as angry as she was and oddly enough, she felt a sort of comforting affinity to him. His next words, however, shocked her to the core and rendered her completely mute. "I'm not planning on running off to Scotland without her. I'm planning on taking her with me." The very air around them seemed to freeze. "As my wife."

Chapter Eight

D EVON BLAKE HAD never and would never claim to be an expert on love or romance or marriage. But even he knew that announcing his intentions to marry Sophia Templeworth to her brother-in-law before actually asking her or even discussing it with her was not the way to go about things.

Especially not with someone as—*forceful*—as the woman currently shooting daggers across the dining table at him. The woman who'd been glaring at him since he'd stupidly blurted out an engagement announcement in the darkened corridor of her sister's house.

Things could not possibly get worse. He looked up to see both Miss Templeworth and the marchioness glaring at him, while Adam looked almost smug as he shook his head in Devon's direction.

Maybe they could get worse. Frankly, he wouldn't put it past the little hoyden across the table to make an attempt on his life. And by all accounts, things would only get worse and infinitely more awkward when the rest of her madcap clan arrived. The worst part of it all was that he knew he was in the wrong.

But he'd panicked. It was as simple as that. He'd been caught unawares. Not just by Adam, but by his own mind. By the feelings that had coursed through him, fierce and unchecked, the second he'd taken Sophia Templeworth in his arms.

The first touch of her lips to his own had ruined him, destroyed all sense of decency and propriety. Destroyed all sense, full stop. He'd completely lost control, and truth be told, he still didn't have a good handle on himself.

He'd known she was beautiful, of course. He'd been attracted to her since that dance they'd shared last year. It was just another plus, he'd told himself. Far better that he find her beautiful than think she resembled a horse's backside. If they were to marry, she would have a duty to his title just as he did. They'd need to produce an heir and a spare at least. So, the fact that she was pretty, well, it had been something of a bonus.

But he couldn't have accounted for how utterly irresistible he would find her once he'd had a taste. He couldn't have imagined that kissing her would spark a desire in him so hot that he was surprised they hadn't melted their very bones.

Christ! He was an experienced man. A *duke*. He knew better than to lose control of himself. Always had done. Since he'd been in leading strings, he'd known the importance of complete self-control. Of self-discipline. When one shouldered the many responsibilities that he did, one didn't have a choice.

One kiss from Sophia Templeworth and he'd been brought crashing to his knees. Self-control be damned. Much as he was loathe to admit it, he knew that it was entirely possible he would have crossed a line if Adam hadn't caught them. And she'd have crossed it right alongside him. That was perhaps the most irresistible thing about her. She had been no shy, retiring debutante in his arms, quaking and fearful. No, she'd been with him every step of the way. He shouldn't have been surprised by her passion, he supposed, since she was a tempestuous little firecracker in every aspect of her life. But it *had* caught him by surprise, and it had been his undoing.

After he'd blurted out that they were getting married there'd been one, horrifying moment of silence before all hell had broken loose. He was surprised she hadn't woken the dead let alone the children with all her caterwauling.

Devon had never heard the language she'd used come from

anyone other than a drunken sailor, and he did wonder at his own sanity for finding it rather entertaining. He'd have stood there like an idiot, still trying to get his body under control, still trying to engage his brain, if she hadn't swung a fist toward him.

A fist! Not a dainty slap, not a quivering palm. No, she'd looked every inch the tiny pugilist as she'd attacked him. Given their height disparity, she only would have landed on his shoulder. And perhaps it would have felt like being hit with a feather. But something about her made him suspicious that though she was diminutive, she would be able to pack quite the punch.

In the end, her sister had intervened and requested there be no blood spilt on the freshly polished floors, so they'd made their way back to the dining room, the sisters whispering furiously together, Adam a silent shadow at his side.

"So," Francesca Templeworth's voice broke the tense silence, causing Devon to jump like a bloody coward and drop his cutlery on his china plate. He scowled at the unladylike snort from across the table. "When are the supposed nuptials taking place?"

Devon opened his mouth to say what he didn't quite know, but he was beaten to it by the little hoyden glaring at him. "Oh, I don't know," she said breezily, though her voice dripped with honey-laced venom. "You'll have to ask the duke, considering it's his fantasy world we're discussing and not reality."

Good Lord, but she was a shrew. His temper flared, and he wondered if he was utterly insane to even be thinking of offering for the woman. But then he remembered how she had felt pressed against him and how much more enjoyable it was to have that tongue of hers engaged in activities other than insulting him.

"I admit that I didn't have a chance to—ah—discuss any plans with Miss Templeworth," he said, studiously ignoring eye contact with Adam.

"Ah, yes. Well, difficult to discuss plans when one is in the throes of a seduction I suppose."

Once again, Devon was rendered speechless. This entire

family was stone mad, he decided. He'd seen glimpses of it last year at the wedding, but that couldn't have prepared him for being on the receiving end of it. And this was only two of them! He wasn't sure he'd survive the lot.

"I wasn't—I mean, I didn't…"

"You were and you did," Adam interrupted, his voice icy. "And it's done now, so we can expedite matters and see about getting a special license. I have a connection in London that—"

"I beg your pardon?"

The sharpness of Sophia Templeworth's tone could cut glass, and they all turned to see her glaring now at Adam. And Devon couldn't help but feel that it was nice to have a break from that glower.

"Sophia, whatever it is you're about to say, please just be reasonable. If people found out about this…"

"They won't." Her tone remained unforgiving, but there was a fire in there now, something that stirred Devon's blood even though it absolutely shouldn't. Not right now.

"You could do a lot worse," Adam said, changing tact. "He's a good man. Usually." Adam spared a death stare for Devon before turning back to Sophia. "And wealthy. He's a *duke* for God's sake. With one of the largest holdings in the peerage. That's not to be sniffed at."

"Yes, well that all sounds great, Adam. But I confess, I found myself singularly unimpressed with the size of his—ah—*holdings*."

It was Devon's turn to scowl as she smiled prettily at him, her sister laughing into her napkin, Adam mumbling under his breath. "I've never had any complaints in that area," he shot back across the table. But if he'd hoped to embarrass or discomfit her, he was sorely disappointed, for she merely raised one, unimpressed brow and stared him down, her blue eyes lit with fire. "I'm sure you haven't," she said. "Dukes tend to attract the sycophants, I'd imagine. I, however, am not one of them, and I will not allow you to announce a betrothal that I didn't and wouldn't agree to."

Devon wanted to answer with a stinging retort equal to her own, but her words gave him pause, and his ire was drowned in a wave of sudden guilt. What the hell was he thinking? She was right. Of course she was. He'd wanted to talk to her, to lay out the proposition of a mutually beneficial marriage. Now that he knew the heat they could create together, he was even surer about the beneficial part.

But he hadn't done that. He'd been caught all over her like a green lad with his first woman and then, rather than be a man about it and apologize, he'd blurted out a marriage announcement without so much as mentioning it in passing to her. It was no wonder she was furious.

He felt a headache begin to form behind his eyes. He'd been here less than twenty-four hours and already felt decades older. And he really wished that they didn't have an audience for this conversation, but there was no way in hell Adam would leave them alone together now, he knew that. And it didn't much seem like the marchioness would leave her sister, either.

He leaned across the table, attempting even the illusion of privacy. Pointless, because in his peripheral vision, he saw both Adam and Francesca lean forward, too.

"You're right," he said softly. "I am so sorry. I know that I behaved abysmally. But I should like to explain myself if you'll give me the chance to."

"Explain yourself? What is there to explain? Just tell Adam you didn't mean it. You were—caught up in the heat of the moment and, and it's all just a misunderstanding."

He should do as she said, Devon knew. Tonight had been an unmitigated disaster. And there was little chance of her agreeing to marry him now in any case. She was far too stubborn for one thing, and far too fiercely independent to allow herself to be forced into matrimony. She was *clearly* unimpressed with his money and his title. And she would no doubt drive him insane. But that kiss. That smart mouth.

"It's not a misunderstanding," he said. "Just terrible timing."

>>>><<<<

SOPHIA FELT HER entire body go numb as she stared across the table at the duke. He was mad. That was the only explanation. He'd gone insane living in that remote part of Scotland of his. What else could explain this?

He hadn't seemed mad when she'd met him last year. And though he'd been quite odious and arrogant up until this point, he hadn't seemed as though he were fit for Bedlam. Yet he must be. For looking into his almost-black eyes she could see not a hint of humor, not a glimpse of mischief.

He truly meant what he said. He was really sitting here telling her that he wanted to marry her! Why, she didn't know. What she did know was that she needed him to stop this nonsense before the rest of her family arrived. For whatever chance she had of convincing Adam not to overreact, there was no way she could convince Gideon—and especially Christian—not to either. They'd have her in front of a reverend before she could blink.

And she didn't even want to think about how Mama would react knowing that he was a *duke* for heaven's sake. His mental deficiencies were going to become her problem if she didn't fix this right now. And it was a crying shame, for her body was still trying to recover from the wicked pleasure he'd awakened in her. If he hadn't been a loon, she might have considered another interlude with him.

"Listen, Your Grace, I'm not entirely sure what sort of game you're playing here but…"

"It's no game," he interrupted. "I think that if you hear me out, you'll agree that it would be in your best interests to agree to marry me."

Just like that, the anger that she'd been desperately trying to keep at bay roared awake inside her. Not only was he addled in the head, but he expected her to be grateful somehow? As though he were doing her some huge favor? Best interests indeed. She felt like smacking him with her roast pheasant.

"My best interests?" she repeated through clenched teeth.

"Exactly," the great big oaf answered patronizingly as though she'd finally gotten her silly head around it. "You wouldn't want to stay here forever, unmarried, and alone, would you? Not when you have the opportunity to be a duchess?"

She couldn't believe it. Quite simply could not believe the man's arrogance, how audaciously he insulted her and then smiled beatifically as though he'd bestowed some great honor on her.

And she *hated* that his words had found their mark. Unmarried, alone, living off the generosity of the men who loved her sisters. She'd already been feeling uneasy about it, but it was infinitely worse to have it pointed out by the condescending swine across the table.

There was so much that she wanted to shout at him. Scream, even. But she didn't think there were enough words in the English language, or any other for that matter, that would adequately convey her rage. And so, she did the only thing that she thought could make her feel even a tad better. She pasted her sweetest smile on her face, then plucked her pheasant from her plate, and threw it straight at him.

And as soon as it smacked him square in the face, she jumped from the table and stormed from the room, Cheska's laughter following her as she went.

Chapter Nine

"**I** MUST ADMIT that when I invited you to stay, I didn't expect you to cause utter havoc within the first twenty-four hours, Farnshire."

Devon winced as Adam's words found their mark. He hadn't expected to cause it either, frankly. Just as he hadn't expected a face full of pheasant at dinner.

"I can only apologize," he said, his voice sounding as uncomfortable as he felt. "You have to know that I would never willingly put you in this position. I just—she just—"

"She's a Templeworth," Adam interrupted wryly. "Believe me, I understand. But Devon." Adam's eyes darkened ominously. "Kissing her senseless in darkened corners of my house? If I didn't hold you in such high regard, you'd have a bullet in you right now. Frankly, I'm still contemplating it."

"I don't blame you," he said. "But if it's any consolation, I highly doubt it will happen again. Not after my unfortunate proposal."

Adam's chuckle eased the tension in the study they were now ensconced in, even if it did make him feel a tad embarrassed.

"You're a damned fool, Farnshire," his friend laughed. "But I can't help feeling sorry for you. When I think of how hard I fell for Cheska, how tormented I was by my feelings for her, well, let's just say I didn't exactly make great decisions at times either."

Devon took the glass of brandy Adam held out to him and

downed the contents in one swallow. He'd had a headache ever since Sophia had weaponized her dinner then run away. He felt guilty that he'd overset her so. Guilty that he'd inadvertently insulted her life. And embarrassed that he'd made such a colossal mess of everything.

"But you and the marchioness are happily married, are you not?" he asked as Adam wordlessly refilled his glass. "You seem to be."

"I couldn't be happier," Adam said, his voice laced with sincerity. "Francesca saved my life. I'll never understand how I got to be so lucky, but there you have it."

Devon's gut twisted at the faint awe in Adam's tone. "You deserve it, my friend," he said. "You truly do."

Adam nodded his gratitude. "For what it's worth, I don't think you had any nefarious intentions with Sophia, and I believe that you've concocted some bizarre but well-meaning plan to marry her. No doubt you feel as though you have good reason. But…" He suddenly grinned at Devon, shaking his head. "What were you thinking?" he finally asked. "If you knew anything about Sophia Templeworth, you'd know that announcing a betrothal and then telling her how privileged she was to be browbeaten into a marriage with you was a sure-fire way to get a pheasant to the face."

"Yes, well, I bloody know that now, don't I?" Devon groused, but he couldn't deny that he felt relieved that they seemed to have moved beyond threats of shootings. "The lass is too damned stubborn for her own good."

"You will do well to remember that telling a Templeworth girl to do *anything* for her own good is akin to signing a death warrant," Adam said wryly. "Especially Sophia. She's always had something of a wildness about her that the others didn't."

"Not even your wife?" Devon asked curiously. From what he'd seen, the marchioness was something of an unconventional lady.

"Not even my wife," Adam confirmed with a laugh. "Francesca wasn't wild, just terrifying. Hope was easily the biggest flirt in Christendom before she married Gideon. And Elodie, well Elodie is a paragon of good-hearted kindness, though she's certainly not to be trifled with. But Sophia? If she could spend her time with horses and never speak to another human being besides her sisters, I think she would be well pleased."

"I should have known that," Devon said with a sigh, staring into his half-empty tumbler. "I *did* know that. It was one of the reasons I wanted to offer for her. You know how I've struggled with Heather and Finn," he continued, glancing up from the glass to see Adam nod solemnly. "I've known the children were unhappy with Mrs. McCluddy for some time now and had meant to find someone better suited to the task. And then I saw them with Miss Templeworth. She managed to get Finn to *smile*, Adam. I can't tell you how that made me feel. And Heather, she's a wild little lass, too. She'd benefit greatly from having a woman with real spirit around."

"Hmm. I'm sure she would," Adam said with a thoughtful frown. "But still, marriage? It seems a bit excessive, Devon."

"Perhaps it is," Devon conceded. "And you know that I don't make rash decisions. I can't afford to. But I am a duke, and I have a duty to the title. I've no inclination to enter the fray of the marriage mart in London, and I've never been one for romance or any of that nonsense. I had a feeling Miss Sophia felt the same."

"She probably does," Adam said. "I've never seen her give more than a fleeting moment of attention to anyone besides my stable hands."

Devon couldn't help his quick smile as he imagined Sophia Templeworth obstinately ignoring everyone and everything that didn't interest her.

"I don't know, I just thought that perhaps she would enjoy the freedom that my title and wealth would afford her."

"I don't think she views marriage as a freedom, Devon. I don't know that any of them would."

"But I wouldn't bother her," Devon argued. "All I would ask

is that she would be there for the children. She would have free reign over my stables and my lands. She could do as she pleased. Wouldn't she want that? If the alternative is a life with her mother, who frankly sounds like a pain in the arse, or marriage to one of the pig farmers she was talking about earlier, isn't the life of a duchess more palatable?"

Adam watched him in silence for what felt like eons before he sighed and sat forward. "Fine," he said. "I'll admit that there actually is merit to this scheme. Sophia has no interest in a Season and only agreed to one to shut her mother up. Her mother who is, as you've surmised, a pain in the arse. So, a conventional marriage is not likely to be on the cards." He squeezed the bridge of his nose. "But equally, you've upset her, and much as I respect you, Devon, I'm not going to stand by and watch you do it again."

"I wouldn't expect you to," Devon assured him.

"And as much as this talk of reason and logic makes sense, it doesn't account for what you were doing with your hands all over her, does it?" There it was—the flash of anger that had been simmering beneath the surface ever since Adam and Francesca had discovered their embrace.

Unbidden, a memory of it flashed through his mind and his cock twitched in response. He pushed it ruthlessly from his head. Now would *not* be a good time for that particular problem to rear its head.

"I—she just—we were…" Never in all his years had he stumbled and tripped over his words like a damned schoolboy in front of an angry tutor. But he couldn't exactly blurt out the truth. Somehow, he didn't think saying "as it happens, I struggle to keep my hands to myself around her and nothing would give me more satisfaction than bedding her" would be well received.

Thankfully, though, Adam seemed to take pity on him for with a wry shake of his head he stood up and moved to once again fill first Devon's glass and then his own. "Ah," he said cryptically. "I see."

"See?" Devon asked. "See what?"

Adam merely shrugged, a sly smile playing across his face.

"Let's just say that you don't have to convince me anymore, my friend." He raised his glass and pointed it in Devon's direction. "But you'll have a hell of a time convincing Sophia."

Devon couldn't supress a groan as he drank deeply before placing the tumbler on the table. "You don't have to remind me," he said, scowling as Adam's laughed bounced around the room.

⇶⟫⟨⟨⟨

"YOU CAN'T IGNORE him for his entire stay, you know."

Sophia pointedly ignored Francesca as she sipped her tea. Just as she'd ignored her last night when she'd come chasing after her as she'd stormed from the dining room.

"You can't ignore me either," Cheska said airily.

Sophia lifted her eyes to glare at her sister before returning them to the table.

"The longer you ignore me, the more likely it is that I shall tell Christian in *detail* what I caught you doing to the poor defenseless duke, you know. Because you might be able to convince Adam and Gideon not to kill him, but we both know Christian is ridiculously protective."

That snapped Sophia's will to remain silent as her sister no doubt knew it would. "I beg your pardon," she bit out. "What *I* was doing to *him*? He's the one who was threatening to marry me!"

"Most people don't consider offers of marriage to be a threat, Sophia."

"Yes, well most people don't hear about it while it's being announced to other people, Francesca," she countered mulishly. "What would you do if a man just decided you were marrying him and told everyone about it?"

"Eviscerate him," Cheska said cheerily.

"Precisely. So, you'll forgive me if I think merely ignoring him is quite generous."

"Hmm. At least you're not planning on throwing any more roasted birds at him."

"There's still time, believe me."

Francesca chuckled appreciatively, and the silence between the sisters grew less tense and more companionable. But then of course, Francesca had to go and ruin it by opening her mouth again.

"You know when Adam came to bed last night..."

"Ugh, please Cheska. I do *not* want to hear about what happened when your husband went to your bedchamber. 'Tis bad enough being around the pair of you when you're in company."

"You have the mind of a wanton, you little hussy," Francesca said airily. "I was merely going to tell you that he spoke with His Grace and, well, he thinks that perhaps you should talk to the duke. Let him explain."

"Oh, he does, does he?"

"Yes," Francesca said, her tone carefully casual. "He does."

"And what do you think?"

"When have you ever cared what I think?"

"Never. But I care even less what Adam thinks, and you've seen fit to share *that* with me."

Cheska sighed and rolled her eyes. "You are stubborn as a mule, Sophia Templeworth. I don't think you should do anything that you don't want to do. I *do* think that there was enough heat between you and the duke to set fire to the entire nursery wing of the house."

Sophia felt her cheeks heat. She who had never blushed a day in her life. It wasn't that she was embarrassed about her kiss with the duke. It wasn't as though Francesca had always been an upstanding lady of decorum and propriety. It was just that every time she thought about it, she felt hot and shivery, that wicked ache she'd discovered in his arms last night a constant reminder of what they'd done.

And she thought about it a *lot*. In fact, part of the reason she was so irritable this morning was that she hadn't had a wink of sleep last night after she'd locked herself away. She'd tossed and turned so much that, in the end, she'd given up on sleep altogether and had been up and dressed in her riding clothes before the birds began to sing.

"Be that as it may," she answered, "I have no interest in marrying the boorish duke, so it really is of no matter what he or Adam or you think."

"Fine. He deserves to be ignored, I suppose. I just thought you might enjoy some more of his company," Cheska said with a wicked grin. "Are you going riding in this? It looks like it will snow soon."

"I won't stay out long," Sophia answered, pleased to be moving the conversation away from confusing talk of the duke. "But snow has never bothered me."

"Are you going to call on Mama?"

"Only if you come with me. Or even better if Adam does. We all know that she won't pay attention to any of us if one of her lords-in-law are around." They shared a conspiratorial grin.

"I'll find some reason to send him over there," Francesca promised. "Maybe I'll even send the duke with him. That should keep her happy until spring."

"Yes, well, as long as he keeps his stupid mouth shut about marrying me, you can send him to the ends of England for all I care. I'll see you later."

"So, if he were to propose again under less—er—*dramatic* circumstances, your answer would be?"

Sophia let her rude gesture speak for her, and judging from Francesca's appreciative laugh, she deemed it answer enough.

Chapter Ten

SOPHIA REINED IN Ares and patted the stallion on his flank as she took in her surroundings. Adam's grounds at Heywood Manor weren't overly large considering it was only a country retreat, but it was big enough for her to have been able to steal his horse this morning and get a decent ride in.

It wasn't even stealing anymore, really, since Adam had given up trying to stop her, and the stable hands were well used to her showing up unannounced and unaccompanied and just taking her pick.

She cast her gaze around the fields that led to the woods bordering the estate. Winter had well and truly made its presence felt, and the snow had fallen thick and heavy. It looked so picturesque that it took her breath away.

She loved the outdoors, regardless of the weather, regardless of the temperature. She would live outside if she could. And usually, she found that time spent in the saddle calmed and relaxed her. But not this morning. No, this morning she was stuck thinking about the duke. And that kiss...

She hated that it had been so earth-shattering, hated that it had rocked her to her core. Hated that she'd never experienced anything like it and was suspicious that she never would again, at least not quite so intensely. She'd never met a man that affected her like that. Not here, not in London. Never. The Fates had a wicked sense of humor, making her yearn for a madman.

Furthermore, she hated how much his words at dinner had affected her. *Hurt* her. Why should she care that he thought her pathetic? That he thought her a lonely spinster? So what if she had had those very same concerns about herself? That still didn't mean it was in any way sane to propose, nay, *announce* a betrothal.

She'd repeated this to herself over and over again as she gave Ares his head and ate up the miles around the estate. Yes, she hated all that. But most of all, she hated that nagging voice in the back of her mind trying to convince her that the idea had some merit. After all, she disliked living at home with a mother determined to foist her off onto anyone who'd take her. And she regretted living off the generosity of her wealthy family. Would it be worse to be living off a husband? The idea of being a duchess of any importance made her go cold, and when she wasn't panting after the duke's giant shoulders or strong jaw like a dog in heat, he got on her very last nerve. And yet, well, she couldn't deny her attraction to the man, inconvenient though it was.

Well, she *would* deny it out loud to her dying breath. But to herself, she could be honest at least.

Perhaps he hadn't meant it. Perhaps he'd been foxed even if he hadn't seemed to be, and he would wake up this morning with common sense, a sore head, and painful regrets.

That idea helped to calm her somewhat, and she heaved a sigh as some of the tension left her shoulders and tried to enjoy the uninterrupted peace of a frosty morning.

"Your sister thought I'd find you here."

Sophia screeched in fright, nearly coming off her horse at the sound of a male voice from behind her, and she turned Ares to see the duke perched upon his own beast, grinning at her.

"Good God lass, you'll wake the dead with that caterwauling."

Sophia ignored the stupid butterflies that tried to dance in her belly at him calling her "lass" and narrowed her eyes suspiciously.

"How's your head this morning?" she asked by way of greeting.

The duke frowned in confusion. "It's fine," he said. "No permanent damage done."

It was Sophia's turn to be confused until she realized he must be talking about the pheasant to the face. He didn't seem upset about it, not if the little smile playing around his mouth was anything to go by. Not that she cared. And she certainly wasn't ashamed of her actions. So, she tiled her chin and held his gaze. "Pity," she sniffed, watching with no small amount of satisfaction as his face dropped.

"What I actually meant was I assume you've sobered up and realized you created a ruckus last night for no reason."

"Ah, I see. It just so happens that's the reason I've sought you out."

"To apologize?" she asked.

"To talk," he countered. They stared each other down for a moment, and Sophia knew that she would sit there and freeze to death rather than be the one to break this odd little stand-off they were in.

Thankfully, though, the duke spoke first. "I do owe you an apology, Miss Templeworth. Sophia," he said, and it did such funny things to her insides to hear her name on his lips. She grew more annoyed with him. "If you'll consent to walking with me for a time, I shall do my best to explain myself, and yes, give you the apology you deserve."

Ordinarily she would have refused just for the sake of it. But she was curious enough to want to hear him explain himself, and of course, there was that nagging voice she'd been trying to ignore. "Fine," she said brusquely. "We can leave the horses by that copse of trees," she said, nodding to where she would usually leave her mount if she was taking a break from riding. "But it's too cold to leave them for long."

"Very well," he agreed easily, dismounting from his giant horse. He turned to assist her, but she rolled her eyes at him and made light work of jumping lithely from Ares's saddle. She felt as his eyes made a slow perusal of her attire: jacket, breeches, and sturdy boots, her hair trailing untied down her back. If Mama knew she was conversing with a duke with untied hair and bedecked in men's clothing, she'd have an apoplexy. But Sophia didn't particularly care what her mother or the duke thought of her attire.

Brushing past him, she headed straight for his glorious stallion, murmuring gently to the horse as she stroked his neck and fed him one of the carrots she kept in her pocket for Ares. The other horse snorted indignantly, and Sophia laughed and held another carrot out so there would be no jealousy between them.

She was still smiling when she turned back to see the duke gazing at her with a look she couldn't quite decipher. "You are incredibly good with horses," he said softly, and she was surprised by how pleased she felt upon hearing his compliment. Worse, she felt her cheeks heat and knew they must be reddening.

"I find horses to be far better company than humans," she said bluntly, surprised once again when he laughed heartily. Those blasted butterflies tried to react to that, too.

"As do I, Sophia," he said easily. She thought about scolding him for the informality of using her given name, but she didn't particularly care and didn't want to seem needlessly petulant. She'd rather reserve her petulance for when she needed it, which she no doubt would if he was going to insist on continuing with that marriage business. "I have a feeling young Finn will be the same."

At the mention of his nephew, the duke's eyes darkened, and Sophia couldn't help feel sorry for the man. She knew something of Lord Farnshire's history with his sister's children. It was such a tragic tale for all of them, and by the looks of vague despair on the duke's face, he felt it keenly.

"He's a wonderful boy," she said gently. "And Heather, well I do believe she has the makings of a Templeworth girl."

At that, his smile returned. "Indeed, she might even be as troublesome as you."

"Me?" She gasped with faux innocence.

"Don't try to play coy with me," he warned. "Adam has filled me in on the antics of you and all your sisters. Your poor brothers-in-law have not a moment's peace with you."

"Your Grace, I assure you, Adam has grossly exaggerated his tales. We are the very picture of ladylike decorum."

"Ah, I see. So, your eldest sister didn't stow away in the viscount's carriage to avoid a marriage?"

"Er—"

"And the other, Hope, was it? She didn't flirt outrageously with the earl when she thought he was a vicar?"

"Well, as to that, there was something of a misunderstanding and—"

"And then, of course, there is the marchioness who chased after Adam and spent the night in an inn with him before they were married?"

Sophia gave up trying to defend herself or her sisters. She wasn't ashamed of them anyway. She had a roaring good time through all of those escapades, and she'd do it all again in a heartbeat. And she certainly wasn't going to allow the duke to make her feel ashamed of herself or her sisters.

"And I have it on excellent authority that you were instrumental in all of these schemes, even as a girl."

"Yes, well. They wouldn't have been able to manage without me," she said with a shrug.

"I well believe it," he answered with a laugh, and Sophia found herself sharing conspiratorial smile with him. It seemed strange to be able to joke with him with everything going on between them and with the memory of the kiss looming. But it was a nice strange. And that just made it all the more confusing.

"Shall we?"

She eyed the arm that the duke held out to her, part of her wanting to run away, part of her wanting so much to hold onto him that she *should* run away until she got some sense. But she didn't run. Instead, she stepped forward and tucked her hand into the crook of his elbow, desperately trying to ignore those determined butterflies.

DEVON FELT AS though he'd won a prize by having Sophia Templeworth not only agree to walk with him but also be rather pleasant. That sharp wit of hers was fiercely entertaining when it wasn't focused on insulting him. She regaled him with tales of her life with her sisters, and Devon found himself wondering how nobody's hair had turned white around them, so hair-raising where their schemes.

As they walked, he could feel the tension ease from her body. He knew that they had weighty things to discuss and yet he found himself unwilling to ruin their unexpected camaraderie.

Instead, he opened up, too, and told her more about the children and how he came to be their guardian. He even surprised himself by confiding in her about his worries for them, his hopes that he could provide them with a happy childhood, his worry that he was failing miserably.

Surprising though it was, considering he'd spent the night being haunted by dreams of her, Devon actually felt quite comfortable in her company, though he was a base enough creature to be utterly distracted by the sight of her in those breeches with her hair falling like a waterfall of chocolate down her back. And she smelled *incredible*. Walking this close to her, he kept getting hints of a tantalizing floral scent mixed with the frosty air around them.

"Are you cold?" he asked, suddenly realizing how much time they'd spent chatting outdoors. And he still hadn't gotten around to the debacle he'd made of his marriage proposal.

"A little," she said with a smile. "But I'm well used to it. We should probably get back to the horses though."

Wordlessly, he turned and led them back in the direction

they'd come from, marveling at how far they'd come, shocked by how distracted he'd been just chatting with her. He hadn't been distracted by anything since his sister had left him in charge of the children. Well, except for last night. Christ, he could barely go five minutes without memories of that kiss. Perhaps now was a good time to bring up the *actual* reason he'd sought her out before he did something foolish like kiss her again.

He knew he had to tread carefully, knew he had to approach such a delicate matter with sensitivity. Especially since she'd proven more than once that she had no qualms about inflicting bodily harm.

Taking a deep breath to steel himself for what was about to come, he turned to face her, trying not to be distracted by how blue her eyes looked in the blinding, winter sun. He opened his mouth to speak, but unsurprisingly, she beat him to it.

"So, I suppose we should talk about this marriage mess you've created, and how we're going to get out of it."

Chapter Eleven

SOPHIA COULD SEE that her frankness took the duke by surprise, but she didn't particularly care. She'd been on tenterhooks since last night, and she'd enjoyed her walk with him so much that it panicked her and made her want to run away.

So, it was best to get this all straightened out now and get on with the business of figuring out what to do with her life. Because if anything had come out of all this, besides a terribly inconvenient attraction to the duke, it was the realization that she couldn't stay like this forever.

She didn't want to marry for anything other than love, and she didn't expect to love anyone, so spinsterhood was most certainly in her future. But staying in Halton with Mama would make her miserable. And living with one of her sisters and encroaching on their family lives was anathema to her. It left her with painfully few options, yes. But at least she could be mistress of her own life. Not a duchess of convenience. Just Sophia Templeworth.

"I admit that I should have handled things better," the duke said, a little shame-facedly. But only a little.

Sophia rolled her eyes. "A *little* better?" she asked.

"Fine," he said with a sigh. "Perhaps a *lot* better. But..." He hesitated, and Sophia's stomach roiled with sudden nerves. "Miss Templeworth... Sophia" he continued, "I am well aware that I behaved appallingly last night. I insulted you when it was not my intention. Though I believe the pheasant was punishment enough," he said wryly, a tiny smile hovering around his lips, "I take it all back," he said, and Sophia cursed herself for a fool for feeling a twinge of disappointment. But before she could respond, he continued. "All except the proposal."

Sophia could only stare at him.

"Though I suppose I didn't actually propose, did I?" he asked drily. "And for that I'm sorry, too. However, I meant what I said, Sophia. I think that we should marry."

She continued to merely stare at him, trying to get her spinning thoughts in order, trying to figure out just what to say to such an outrageous statement. But staring into his black-as-sin eyes, her brain seemed to have become the consistency of the snow melting beneath her boots. "But why?" she managed to croak.

He opened his mouth, closed it again, opened it and then issued a string of black expletives before sighing, the sound coming from the depths of his soul. "I have—certain obligations," he said stiltedly. "A duty to my title. A duty to marry. I knew it, and yet I never particularly gave a damn. Er, excuse the language."

She managed a snort. "That's hardly the worst language I've heard. Or used, come to think of it."

"I have no doubt," he laughed.

"With all due respect, Your Grace, I'm not really sure what any of this has to do with me."

"I'm getting there," he answered swiftly, and for some reason that annoyed her.

"Do you think you might get there before we all freeze to death?" she asked.

"Christ, you're difficult, lass," he growled.

"Precisely. So, let's just leave it there, and we can both just forget about all this silliness."

"I don't want to forget it," he insisted stubbornly.

Sophia gritted her teeth, suddenly feeling as though she were dealing with one of her stubborn nephews and not a grown man.

"You know, no one in my life has ever truly gotten under my skin until you, Miss Templeworth. Or even come close to it."

"Well, there's a first time for everything, is there not?"

Sophia got the distinct impression that he wanted to swear some more. But he didn't. He merely raised his eyes to the heavens, muttering something under his breath about impossible women before facing her again, this time his dark eyes blazing with emotion.

"I'm terrified that I'm going to ruin those children's lives," he blurted, shocking her with the raw honesty in his tone. "And I don't want to just hire another governess, another nanny. They deserve someone who cares about them. They deserve, they deserve a mother. And I know that we barely know each other, and you have no reason to accept what must seem like a rather insane proposal. But I have thought about this, despite appearances, and I think we would both benefit from the arrangement."

Sophia was almost certain she'd lost the ability to speak. She'd never seen him speak so impassionedly. Though to be fair, she barely knew the man, which was a huge part of the problem. But that passion—well, she'd experienced it elsewhere, hadn't she? Perhaps she hadn't *heard* him be impassioned, but she'd certainly felt it in his kiss, his touch. But that was hardly relevant.

However, something of what she was feeling must have shown in her face, for his expression suddenly became positively wolfish, and it took all her strength and stubbornness not to back away from the predatory glint in his eyes.

"I'd be more than happy to demonstrate some of those benefits now," he growled, and a shiver—that had nothing to do with the frosty air and everything to do with the molten lava that pooled in her gut—wracked her body. But she couldn't let him see that he had this effect on her. Couldn't let him win this battle of wills.

"As far as I know, you don't need to be married to enjoy those *benefits*," she answered tartly, her voice not quite as steady

A WINTER WEDDING

as she would have liked. "And I'm positive that you haven't married every woman you've bedded."

Her cheeks heated at the flash of fire in his dark eyes. "How do you know how many women I've bedded?" he challenged, and Sophia wished she'd never started down this bloody road.

"You're a wealthy, handsome duke," she said, rolling her eyes. "And arrogant beyond reason. It's not hard to guess that you've had women throwing themselves at you. Odds are that you've chosen to catch at least some of them." She could tell that she'd shocked him, and she hoped that would be the end of this ridiculousness. But apparently, she'd underestimated him.

"Well, at least you think I'm handsome," he answered with that infuriatingly charming grin.

But she was in no mind to be charmed. Especially when all that talk of bedding women had made her feel all funny inside. If she didn't know better, she'd think that she was envious, which was utterly ridiculous of course.

"Tell me, why are you so adverse to marrying me?"

He couldn't be serious! "B-because I don't *know* you," she spluttered. "Because I have no interest in or intention of marrying anyone, least of all an arrogant lord who thinks he can just announce it as a *fait accompli*."

He opened his mouth, no doubt to rile her further, but she didn't want to give him the opportunity. "And because contrary to what you might think of my circumstances, they are not so dire as to force me to wed a man who wants nothing more from me than to be a glorified nanny for the children in his care."

She turned on her heels and made to march back to the horses, but she hadn't made it more than two steps before his hand reached out and grasped her upper arm, spinning her until she was facing him again.

"I want more than that," he gritted.

"Oh really?" she drawled sarcastically. "Like what?"

"Like this," he growled before grasping the back of her neck and pulling her head toward his in a ferocious kiss.

77

Chapter Twelve

DEVON KNEW THAT he needed to stop manhandling the lass. But Christ, she made it difficult. Every time he was near her, he wanted her. Ordinarily that would be a fairly enjoyable problem to have with one's betrothed. Only the little hoyden still wouldn't agree to it.

He'd yet to have a rational conversation with her about it. Because every time he tried to engage his brain around her, his good sense was overrun by other, more demanding parts of his anatomy, and he was lost.

He hadn't meant to kiss her. And he sure as hell hadn't meant to confess his fears about the children to her. But he was coming to learn that when it came to Sophia Templeworth, he had no control over himself. And he needed to get some. Fast. Or he'd end up tupping her right there in the snow.

And he was about to pull back from her. He really was. Until her arms suddenly snaked around his neck, her tiny fingers pulling at his hair. And what tiny vestige of control he had snapped completely. Growling into her mouth, he lifted her from her feet, his cock jumping as she wrapped her breeches-clad legs around his waist, her tongue meeting every thrust of his own.

He moved them the few paces to the tree where the horses were tethered. The sound that came out of her mouth when her back connected with the trunk nearly brought him to his knees, and he surged against her, the kiss becoming savage as the fire between them raged.

Keeping one hand on her hip, Devon moved the other to tangle in her hair, angling her head to deepen their kiss, before wrenching his mouth from hers to press against the silken skin of her throat. The scent of her skin drove him beyond reason, and he knew she was just as caught up in the madness as he was, for every kiss, bite, and lick was met with a surge of her hips, a tightening of her legs around his waist.

"This, Sophia," he whispered against her neck, pushing himself into the cradle of her hips, delighted in the gasp he wrung from her lips. "This is what I want. What you want. This is what we can have if you're mine."

He might as well have doused her in cold water for the impact the words had on her. He felt her entire body freeze momentarily before she was pushing against his shoulders. She might as well have been a kitten for all the effect her shoving had on him, but he let her go immediately, lowering her to her feet and stepping back from her on legs that weren't entirely steady.

"Did you really think you could seduce me into saying yes?" she snapped, though he noted with no small amount of satisfaction that she was as breathless as he felt.

"I just thought to demonstrate one of the many reasons that this could be a good thing, Sophia."

"You are ridiculous," she said. "I haven't given you leave to use my name, so don't do it. And as for that particular *benefit,* I'm sure I could find a willing volunteer to..."

"Don't." He surprised even himself with that little outburst, but he couldn't help it, just as he couldn't help the sudden but intense burst of jealously that coursed through him at even the idea of another man's hands on her.

What the hell is going on, he asked himself. *Why do I even care?*

He was beginning to wonder if this was a good idea when a shout sounded behind them, and he turned to see Finn and Heather racing toward him through the snow. The usual feeling of nervousness settled in the pit of his stomach, but on its heels came confusion. What were they doing out here alone? Where the hell was Mrs. McCluddy? And why couldn't he just have a bloody rational conversation with the stubborn chit beside him without being interrupted or allowing his desire to get the better of him?

Cursing under his breath, he began to stride toward the children, his heart thundering, and his blood boiling as he saw that they weren't properly attired for the winter. They must be freezing. Without a backward glance at the woman driving him to Bedlam, he hurried down the hill toward his niece and nephew. "Finn, lad. What are you doing out here and with your sister?"

Even from this distance he could see that the children seemed overset, both of their tiny bodies shivering whether that be with cold or upset he couldn't tell. But it was enough for him to know that something was wrong, and as panic seized him, he bolted toward them. Sophia and her strange hold on him quite forgotten.

It didn't take long for him to cross the distance to his niece and nephew but when he was in front of them, he froze, wanting to scoop them up but unsure if he should. And because he felt so uneasy, his voice came out a lot harsher than he intended as he dropped to a knee in front of the shaking children. "What happened?" he demanded, the words sharper than he'd intended, and guilt clawed at his gut as he watched his nephew flinch. Heather however, who'd just now caught up to her brother, didn't appear afraid.

"Mrs. McCluddy is sick," his niece said. "And... and..."

"Heather, hold your whist," Finn said with a scowl. "Uncle Devon doesn't want to be bothered." Devon could only stare at the lad, shame and guilt twisting in his gut. He wanted to tell Finn that it wasn't true. Wanted to demand to know why the boy thought that way. But he couldn't seem to form the words.

There was a horrible silence that seemed to stretch for eons, and Devon had no clue how to break it. But before he could even figure it out, there was Sophia's lilting voice from behind him.

"And what do we have here? Two runaways. How marvelously exciting." Devon could only watch on, mute and uncomfortable, as she sank to her knees, unbothered by the cold, wet ground. "Are you up to something naughty then?"

Heather giggled, and even Finn looked like he might smile, but the expression was gone before it had fully formed.

"Mrs. McCluddy is sick," Heather repeated to Sophia, her eyes wide. "She said that her head hurt and we needed to be quiet. But…" She paused, looking warily at Finn, whose eyes were trained on the frosty ground, his cheeks scarlet. "But Finn dropped his cup of milk and it splashed on her d-dress." To Devon's horror, the little one's eyes filled with tears, and her lip began to quiver. He'd break out in a cold sweat if she cried. He couldn't stand to see crying. Especially from an innocent little girl. "She struck him," Heather whispered, but the words roared through Devon, awakening a rage so white hot he was surprised it hadn't melted the skin from his bones.

"She *what*?"

Devon, being six feet, five inches of solid, Highland muscle had never feared anyone or anything in his life. But damned if the fury in Sophia Templeworth's voice didn't make him feel like taking a step away from her. And when she turned those eyes on him, when he saw the cobalt fire in their depths, he reached up to loosen his suddenly too tight cravat. And he wasn't even the one in trouble!

"She said he was naughty and that he would be ruined without a mother or father to–to teach him how to behave. And then sh-she struck him and told us we weren't to bother Uncle Devon about it."

Everything in Devon's head went completely silent. Everything simply emptied out of him. And then when the rage returned, it wasn't burning as it had been. It was ice cold. A band of steel wrapped around his heart and mind until he felt as though his entire body was made up of nothing but cold, hard fury. And he who had prided himself on never harming a hair on a woman's head was ready to kill that poisonous old trout for what she'd done to these children. For the cruel, despicable things she'd said to them.

He took a step back from the children and their sniffling, away from Sophia and her anger. Then another and another. He was going to wring her scrawny neck. Without a word, he turned from Sophia and the children, some intrinsic part of him trusting her to take care of them. Before he'd taken more than a couple of steps, however, he felt her small hand on his arm. It wouldn't have taken even half a thought to shrug her off, yet she brought him to a halt all the same.

He turned his head to look down at her, seeing her own anger still shining in her eyes, but there was concern there, too, and wariness.

"None of that is true," she said to the children, her hand still on Devon's arm. "Your uncle is never too busy for you. In fact, he was just telling me that he was going to fetch you both so you could..." He watched her eyes dart around the grounds dusted with snow. "So you could collect holly berries and garlands to decorate the house for the marchioness."

Devon gaped at her, then turned to see the children gaping at *him*. He didn't blame them. It would never in a million years dawn on him to take the children berry picking for God's sake. Yet looking into their little faces, seeing the remnants of their tears, seeing Finn's dark eyes look so forlorn, he couldn't say no.

Gritting his teeth against the irritation he felt at having to stay out here and let that damned McCluddy woman get away with her behavior, he turned what he hoped was a sincere smile on the children. "Miss Templeworth is absolutely right," he said a little weakly. "But first we must return to the house and get your cloaks and winter boots."

And though he'd been annoyed at getting strong-armed into this, seeing the genuine joy on the children's faces at such a simple act made him feel as though he'd won some sort of prize he'd never even known he wanted. That still didn't explain the actions of the woman beside him, however.

He hurriedly instructed the children to run to the horses, then turned to face the interfering miss. She blinked up at him, those huge eyes bluer than a summer's sky, but he refused to be fooled by the innocence in them. Just as he refused to find her interfering charming.

"And while I'm out here hunting holly berries, what exactly are you going to do?" he groused through his teeth.

The forced innocence on her face grew even more pronounced. "Me?" she said airily. "Oh, nothing much. I'm just going to kill your nanny."

SOPHIA DIDN'T KNOW what to expect from the duke, but it wasn't laughter. Yet that's exactly what happened. His mouth dropped open as though she'd shocked him to his very core, and then suddenly he burst into a peal of laughter that rang out over the snowy grounds.

And to her horror, those bloody butterflies fluttered in her belly at the sound. She really would have to do something about them.

"What's so funny?" she asked, hating that she felt so discomfited. Hating that a tiny part of her wished that the children hadn't interrupted them. Wished that Lord Farnshire would finish what he started. Even now, even with fury at that odious old dragon boiling her blood, she was remembering how his eyes had darkened with jealousy as they'd argued, how his huge body had pressed her so forcefully into that tree, the growls that had vibrated against the skin of her neck. And it hit her like a runaway carriage, she was in very real danger here. The duke would be trouble. Already was.

"Nothing, lass," he said, making her knees turn to the consistency of treacle. "But if I can't go after the old crow, then you can't either." She opened her mouth, then shut it, not quite knowing what to say.

Finally, she settled on berating him. "So, you're just going to allow her to say those horrid things and *hit* that poor little boy and do nothing," she hissed in deference to the little ears that would surely hear if she yelled as she wanted to.

"No, I'm not," the duke answered softly. And something about that low tone made a shiver of apprehension skate down her spine. For only a complete dolt would fail to see the murderous rage stamped on his face. "And I would be dealing with her right now, only a certain somebody told my niece and nephew that I want to pick damned Christmas decorations with them."

She held herself still lest her body start to squirm under that intense gaze. "I thought that perhaps they needed to spend some time with you, to disprove what she'd said," Sophia admitted, not used to explaining herself to anyone. Certainly not used to *wanting* to explain herself. Yet here she was. Explaining. Some emotion that she couldn't quite place flickered through his eyes. He almost looked scared. And her heart twisted. "Perhaps you need it, too," she ventured, half expecting him to rail at her and stomp off.

But she was remembering what he'd confessed before he'd kissed her and turned her entire world on its head. How frightened he was for those children. How scared he was that he couldn't be what they needed. Yes, this was important for all of them. And though she'd insisted that she wanted nothing to do with him, though she'd been determined to keep her distance from him, she couldn't help yearning to make things better for all of them.

He ran a hand through his black hair, ruffling it into a disarray that rather unfairly made him seem even more ruggedly handsome. Finally, he sighed. "Och, you're probably right," he said, that Scottish brogue even more pronounced. "I can deal with Mrs. McCluddy later."

"Or," she ventured, still feeling furious with the drunken woman, "I can go and deal with her now."

His answering grin was a thing of sheer, unadulterated beauty, and Sophia's breath caught at the sight of it. "Patience, little hellcat," he said, causing her very bones to heat. "She'll be dealt with. But not now."

"And why is that?"

"Because you are picking holly branches with us."

"Me? Why?"

To her shock and, yes delight, he reached out and ran his thumb along her neck, just above her collarbone. "Because I don't trust you not to murder her where she stands," he said gruffly. "And this neck is far too beautiful to hang from any gallows."

He'd already reached the children and the horses before Sophia remembered to breathe.

Chapter Thirteen

"NOW, JUST THREAD the ribbon through it, and yes! Well done, Heather. A perfect wreath." Sophia laughed as Heather jumped up and down, squealing with excitement. Beside where they were sitting cross-legged on the floor, Finn was busy twisting and shaping his own garland. Though he was a lot more subdued than his sister.

Sophia had done her best to distract the children while Lord Farnshire had disappeared. They'd spent a surprisingly pleasant few hours hunting down berries and greenery to make Heywood Manor more festive. Not that it had been necessary, for Francesca would have ensured the house was bedecked in yuletide splendor. Sophia had only suggested it because the duke had been floundering in the face of the children's upset, and her heart had hurt to see it.

That and the fact that she'd wanted the children out of the way while she dealt with that horrible creature, Mrs. McCluddy. She kept wondering why she cared so much about children she barely knew. About a man she barely knew. But she didn't like how uncomfortable that made her feel, so she ignored it as she did most things that made her uneasy.

It had done the children a world of good to spend time away from that odious woman and have Lord Farnshire's attention solely on them. And it had also done the duke some good, Sophia reminded herself, to be out of the house. To see that the children wanted and needed him around.

And as she'd watched him grow more comfortable with them, laughing at Heather's excitement or gently teaching Finn how to safely cut the boughs from bushes and trees, she found herself considering the duke's proposition, imagining a lifetime of this—teaching and laughing and being right in the center of a family life instead of on the outskirts of it.

She wasn't entirely thrilled by how appealing it was. Especially when she caught the duke watching her with that darkly intense gaze that set her to imaging what other things she could experience if she married him.

"This is what I want. What you want. This is what we can have if you're mine."

Those words whispered so seductively while she'd been in his embrace danced through her head, and she ruthlessly pushed them away. Bad enough that she'd spent the afternoon with them flitting around her head. She didn't need to obsess over them now, too.

"Here we are." The door to the drawing room swung open to reveal Francesca carrying a handful of candles and red ribbon, followed by an army of servants laden down with even more supplies.

A maid with a tray of cider and ginger biscuits brought up the rear, and Sophia laughed as both children dove on the treats. She stood up to take a seat on the chaise beside her sister, realizing that she'd have to change for dinner soon.

While the children ate and argued over the ribbons, she quickly filled Francesca in on what had occurred that morning with the children and their horrid nanny.

"That explains Devon thundering through the house like a bull," Cheska said, her eyes so like Sophia's, wide with speculation. "My housekeeper Mrs. Philips was beside herself when she came running into me. Said the duke looked fit to kill Mrs. McCluddy and had ordered her to be packed up and out by the dinner hour. Apparently, she'd squealed and squawked like a farm animal, but the duke hadn't cared. Said she could walk back to Scotland for all the damn he gave about her."

Sophia felt a little thrill of shock go through her. Though she'd seen the duke's anger for herself, she hadn't really known what he would do when they'd finally returned to the house. He'd left them all in the drawing room, asking them to start without him while he took care of something and then with nothing more than a speaking look to Sophia, he'd hurried out.

"Has she left?" she whispered to Francesca, who was watching the children with a soft smile on her face.

"Hmm? Oh, yes. I believe even you might have backed down in the face of such wrath. Adam saw to it that she had a carriage and an escort back to Farnshire. I think Devon was too angry to do it, but Adam said the duke would have an attack of conscience if he'd really left the old trout to her own devices."

Sophia turned to watch the children. "How could she strike a little boy like that?" she asked softly, more to herself than to her sister. "How could she say such an awful thing to children who've already lost so much?"

Francesca didn't answer for a while, then she sighed. "I don't know," she said. "But I feel for them. And Devon, too. I can tell that he's a good man, but there seems such a distance between them all. Perhaps he's right, Sophia. Perhaps they do need a mother. Perhaps he does need a wife to help him navigate all of this."

Immediately, Sophia stiffened. "I'm sure he does," she said. "But that's none of your business. Or mine."

Francesca merely rolled her eyes and nudged her shoulder. "That's not what it looked like when you were wrapped around him last night," she laughed.

"Yes, well. I seem to recall a lot of your own wrapping in this very house when you were very much single."

"But I married my one," Cheska countered. "And by the way, Hope married hers *and* Elle married hers so..." She trailed off with a shrug.

"Thankfully, your stupidity isn't catching," Sophia sniffed, though in truth, she thought her sisters had all married exactly whom they should. But they'd married for the right reason. For love. True, life-changing love. And though she was the furthest thing from a romantic, though she far preferred the company of horses to humans, she didn't think she'd ever be able to bring herself to enter some sort of business arrangement just so that she didn't have to be a spinster.

"You don't really think I should consider this, do you?" she asked her sister. "There's absolutely no reason why I would."

Francesca studied her in silence for a moment or two before she opened her mouth to speak. But before she got the chance to, Heather appeared and clambered into Sophia's lap and rested her head on her like she was meant to be there. The action caused Sophia's heart to twist. Finn hurried over, too, and triumphantly held up a candle that he'd smothered in ribbon and holly berries, his shy little smile making her want to weep.

And then the door opened, and in walked the duke, his eyes homing in on her straight away and, yes, there went the flurry of inconvenient and unwelcome butterflies.

She felt as though time stood still as the duke gazed at her, and try as she might, she couldn't pull her eyes from him. She was caught completely and utterly in his thrall. So focused on the duke was Sophia that she didn't notice Francesca had leaned toward her, until she heard her sister's maddening voice whisper in her ear. "Oh, I can think of a reason why you would."

DINNER THIS EVENING had been a far less dramatic yet more enjoyable affair than the night before, Devon mused as he sat nursing a tumbler of brandy in Adam's library. All around him was evidence of his afternoon with Sophia and the children.

His lips quirked as he took in the garlands and the difference in them. Some neat as a pin, some so haphazard that they could have only been done by the hands of children. He was still feeling that deep, comforting happiness that he'd felt this afternoon despite the ugly scene with Mrs. McCluddy. And though his anger really knew no bounds, he was glad that Adam had arranged transport for the older woman. Despite what she'd done, he couldn't have in good conscience allowed a woman to travel alone.

His gut clenched with guilt and something undefinable as he remembered how shocked and pleased the children had been when he'd come into that drawing room and told them that Mrs. McCluddy wouldn't be around anymore. Wee Heather had even thrown her tiny arms around his leg before scurrying back to Sophia on the chaise. Damned if hadn't gotten a lump in his throat at the simple, innocent gesture.

Lady Heywood had kindly assigned a young maid to take care of the children until he got back to Scotland and hired someone more suitable. Though he still hoped that he would return with a wife and not a governess or nanny.

Just like that, his thoughts drifted straight back to Sophia Templeworth. Not that they were ever far from her. Christ, he couldn't seem to get her off his mind. Not that he tried very hard. Truth be told, she was starting to consume almost all of his thoughts.

It was bizarre, and in all honesty, he wasn't entirely pleased about it. When he'd decided he wanted to marry her, it had been for solid, logical reasons. He'd never intended to become wrapped up in her. Yet after only a few days, he was in very real danger of just that. Sighing, he downed the rest of his brandy and made quick work of pouring another.

The fire in the hearth crackled, warding off the frost already gathered on the windowpanes. The sky outside was clear, allowing the moon to cast an icy glow on the snow all around the manor house. It was beautiful. Just as Christmas should be. The children would no doubt enjoy the snow, and Sophia had promised to take them skating on the pond tomorrow if it was safe. No, he corrected himself with a smile, she'd promised them that *he'd* take them to the pond to skate tomorrow.

And the most surprising thing of all wasn't that this slip of a girl felt at ease ordering a duke about, but that he was actually looking forward to doing her bidding. Shaking his head a little, he downed his drink yet again. Something to take the edge off, he told himself. Something to help him sleep because he sure as hell hadn't managed to do so, not without being haunted by visions of the woman who didn't want him.

He scowled as he remembered her talk of finding some *willing* man to satisfy her, that heated jealousy roaring to life inside him. And the fact that he wanted to rip that non-existent man limb from limb with his bare hands was proof that the woman was driving him mad.

The door to the library creaked open, and his heart stopped dead in his chest. There she was, as though his desire to see her had conjured her. His eyes roved over her, greedily taking in every detail. The waterfall of chestnut waves, the huge blue eyes, the silhouette of her body that he could see through the thin material of her night rail. Earlier she'd been dressed in an ice-blue satin gown that had made her look uncommonly pretty. Now, she looked heartbreaking.

Devon suddenly realized that he was still sitting and looking less than well put together. He jumped to his feet, casting his eyes around for the jacket and cravat he'd discarded, yet seeing neither.

"Couldn't sleep?" he asked for want of anything better to say.

"No. I was looking for…"

"A book, I assume. To help you nod off?" Why else would she be in the library after all?

"As it happens, I know Adam stashes some of his good brandy in here. And it appears you've found it."

Devon felt his jaw drop. "You—you came in here looking for brandy?" he asked, incredulous.

"So?" He watched her chin tilt up in what he was coming to learn was quite a regular occurrence for him. "You did, too."

He huffed out a laugh. "So I did," he answered, moving toward the half empty bottle and pouring her a healthy measure of it. He didn't know why he was surprised that she drank brandy. Of course she did. There was absolutely nothing conventional about this woman. For his sanity, he should remember that more often.

Turning with her glass filled and his own replenished, he watched as she sat in the chaise by the fire, tucking her feet under her, giving him a tantalizing glimpse of delicately muscled calves. His cock twitched at even that infinitesimal glance, and he gritted his teeth against the desire to grab hold of her. He hadn't felt this controlled by his hormones since he'd been a lad of thirteen, for God's sake.

Handing over her tumbler, he took a seat on the opposite end of the chaise, though it was so small that he was practically pressed against her, and he couldn't help notice the hitch in her breath as his thigh brushed against her legs.

The air between them fairly crackled.

"I hope you can skate," he said, his voice gravelly from the desire he was keeping a desperate leash on.

She blinked at him before smiling a mischievous little smile that had him clenching a fist to stop from tracing the action with his thumb. "I can, actually," she said. "But what does that have to do with anything?"

"You volunteered me to skate," he answered. "That means you skate, too. Just like the berry picking."

She huffed out a breathless laugh, and Devon already knew that he was going to lose the battle against his willpower. He put his glass on the table before the fireplace, reaching out and wordlessly taking her own to do the same.

"I don't remember agreeing to that or even discussing it," she said haughtily, but he saw the pulse hammering at the base of her throat and knew that she wasn't as unaffected by him as she'd like him to believe. "And I didn't say I was finished with that drink."

"You volunteered my time, Miss Templeworth," he said as he ran his eyes lazily over her. "So, I volunteer yours. I'd say that's only fair, wouldn't you?"

"Well, unfortunately for you, I don't particularly care about being fair," she answered huskily.

He reached out and rubbed his thumb against her hammering pulse, watching in fascination as her skin turned that maddening shade of pink. "Are you scared to spend the day with me, Sophia?" he asked, inching closer until there was barely a breath between them.

She rolled her eyes, but he didn't buy the nonchalance. Not for a moment. "I'm not scared of anything," she muttered, her eyes on his mouth playing havoc with his senses.

"You're scared of me," he countered smoothly. "What you feel for me. What I do to you. How your body reacts to mine."

Her eyes narrowed dangerously, but that fluttering pulse, that labored breathing—they gave her away.

"I told you, I'm not scared of anything," she reiterated, and he smirked at her knowing that she was as close to the precipice as he was.

"Prove it," he dared.

Time seemed to freeze as they stared each other down. And then, she snapped. With a feminine little growl, she reached out and grabbed hold of his lawn shirt, pulling him forward and pressing her lips firmly against his own.

Chapter Fourteen

S OPHIA KNEW DAMN well she'd allowed herself to be manipu-
lated into this kiss, but the second her lips made contact with
his, she didn't care. At the first touch, she went up in flames. And
when he took control of the embrace, reaching out and pulling
her onto his lap, plunging his tongue inside her mouth to dance
with her own, she conceded to him immediately.

It became less about proving or disproving anything and just
about the pleasure he drew from every fiber of her being.

With a masculine growl that went right to the core of her,
Devon's hands wrapped around her thighs, and in one swift
movement, he had her straddling him, the rigid length of him
pressed against her. Sophia couldn't contain her moan at the
contact, as the dart of pleasure she felt as her hips moved of their
own accord.

"Christ, lass. You'll be the death of me," he groaned against
her mouth, even as he grabbed her hips and pulled her even
closer.

Sophia couldn't think. And she didn't want to. Moving on
instinct alone, she plunged her hands into his dark, silken hair and
held on as his own hands went on a slow, torturous journey of
her body. They glided from her hips, scorching a path up her
back, the heat of them intense through the soft, thin material of
her night rail.

Sophia gasped as his hand cupped her aching breast, and she

pushed herself further into his palm, wordlessly demanding more. He huffed a laugh against her mouth before pulling his mouth away from pressing against her neck, licking at the pulse that was hammering at the base of her throat.

Every one of his actions resulted in torturous pleasure, and still she wanted more. There was a dark, wicked ache demanding to be sated, and it grew with every brush of his hand, every stroke of his tongue. And then, that hand moved again, plunging inside her nightgown, and drawing a cry of pleasure from her lips. The feel of his callused, heated skin against her own was almost unbearable, and her hips surged in response, drawing a tortured groan from the duke's lips.

"Please," she panted, all sense of pride gone as she gave herself over to the man between her legs. Some tiny part of her knew she shouldn't be doing this. But that part was having a lot less fun than the rest of her, so she ignored it. She didn't even know what she was begging for, she only knew that if he didn't do something about this *need* growing inside her, she would explode.

"I know, lass," he whispered against her throat before he took her lips again, swallowing every moan, every gasp, every whimper.

He kept that clever hand on her breast, teasing her nipple into a hard peak. And then his other hand drifted over her hip, around the skin exposed by the nightgown that had ridden up around her waist. And her breath, her very heart stopped dead as it moved around her hip, and his fingers brushed against her once, twice, before parting her and finding the very center of her need.

Sophia cried out once more as the pad of his thumb found a secret, magical spot at the apex of her thighs, pressing against it until she was frantic, until she was climbing higher and higher, desperately rushing toward something that she wasn't sure she'd survive. And just when she knew she couldn't take anymore, he plunged a long, thick finger inside of her, stretching her and sending her shooting into the stars in an explosion of feeling.

She pushed herself shamelessly against his hand, riding out

the storm of bliss, and Devon stayed with her every step of the way, stroking and soothing until she collapsed against him, her body shaking from the intensity of what he'd done to her.

Sophia pressed her head against him, her face buried in his neck, inhaling the oaky, masculine scent of him, trying to put the pieces of herself back together. Only when she was sure that she'd have the strength to hold her head up did she move, lifting her head and inadvertently pressing herself closer to him, eliciting a hiss of pain.

She snapped her eyes open in horror, afraid that she'd hurt him somehow, and when she took in the look of agony on his face, she knew that she must have. "I-I'm sorry," she gasped, trying to pull herself from his lap, but that only seemed to pain him further, and his hands clamped down on her waist, holding her still.

"Hell and damnation," he rasped. "Stop. Moving."

Sophia stilled and watched as he heaved a breath, then another, before finally opening his eyes. The heat in their depths stole her breath clean out of her body.

"I need a minute," he said roughly. "Just–hold still."

"B-but aren't I hurting you?" she whispered, earning herself a choked laugh.

"Aye," he said, still in that agonized tone. "But not in the way you think."

And suddenly it dawned on Sophia just what he meant. Her gazed down to the impressive if a little intimidating bulge visible in his breeches. "Oh," she said, and he choked out another pained laugh.

"Indeed," he said ruefully. "This is what you do to me just breathing the same air, lass. So you cannot imagine how glorious it was to witness you come undone under my hands."

"But you didn't–I didn't..." she trailed off, embarrassment scalding her cheeks. "You didn't enjoy..."

"Oh, believe me, I did," he interrupted gruffly. "Which is why we're in this predicament."

She giggled at the seriousness in his tone, earning herself a playful scowl. "It's not funny," he groused. "I won't be able to move for a week at this rate."

It dawned on Sophia that she probably shouldn't feel this comfortable, this *giddy* around the duke after what they'd just done. And especially with that silly proposal hanging over their heads. Yet she did. For the first time in her adult life, she felt entirely, blissfully at ease with a gentleman. Felt safe and exhilarated all at once. And knowing that gave her the confidence to smile wickedly at him, to lean forward and press the whisper of a kiss against his lips. "Well, we can't have that," she said as she moved her hand slowly down the rock-hard muscle of his chest and abdomen, stopping at the ties of his breeches. "Not if we're to go skating tomorrow."

His eyes darkened to coal black, a growl rumbling through his giant chest. "No," he said. "We cannot."

"So, then, let's do something about it," she said boldly.

His mouth crashed into her own again even before she'd finished getting the words out, and he reached down to grab hold of her hand and press it against the length of him. She flexed her hand, and he dropped a black oath inside her mouth.

Sophia felt a thrill at how much power she had over him. How she could evoke such a reaction in one so forceful as he. Guided by instinct and led by the sounds of needy pleasure she drew from him, she moved her hand, dipping it into his breeches to wrap around the length of him. The touch made him savage, and he lifted her from his lap, dropping her onto her back on the chaise and looming over her.

He broke their kiss, not to move away from her but to drop his eyes to her hand, to watch as she stroked him. He reached down, his hand covering hers as he guided her motions, setting a rhythm that seemed to drive him out of his mind. Sophia miraculously felt her own body begin to climb toward that peak of pleasure once more as she watched him come undone under her touch. Devon seemed to sense it, too, for he suddenly reached out and found that secret bundle of nerves with an expert touch. And by the time he went over the edge, growling into her neck, she flew over right along with him.

DEVON DIDN'T KNOW how long he lay there sprawled across the too-small chaise with Sophia's delectable body lying right on top of him. He toyed with one of her curls, rubbing the satiny lock between his fingers and inhaling the floral scent as he pressed his lips to the crown of her head.

Nothing could have prepared him for seeing her fall apart in his arms, for feeling that delicate hand wrapped around the length of him. She might be an innocent, naïve in the ways of lovemaking, but she was sure as hell a fast learner.

"Sophia?" He spoke softly in deference to the quiet night, and because he was hesitant to break this magical spell that seemed to have weaved its way around them.

"Hmm?" She sounded sleepy and satiated, and Devon's heart squeezed with the oddest sensation of tenderness.

"Marry me," he whispered.

"No," she whispered back with no hesitation. But instead of angering him, it made him laugh.

"Well, it was worth a try." He felt her huff of laughter against his neck and figured it was progress of sorts.

The silence stretched on for a few moments longer as another idea formed in his head.

"Very well," he said, sitting up and pulling her up with him. He set her away from him because he knew he wouldn't be able to concentrate on forming a coherent sentence if she was still attached to him. "I have a new proposal."

She eyed him warily, and he really did try not to find it adorable. She would be furious, he knew, to be called something so sweet.

"We have three weeks until I leave for Scotland," he said. "And when I leave, I want to be leaving with you as my wife. Or," he hurried on when it looked as though she'd interrupt, "at least as my betrothed."

"You m-phm." He watched her eyes grow wide, then narrow ominously as he reached out and covered her mouth with his palm.

"I have gone about this in the most incorrect way possible," he continued, keeping his hand where it was because he wanted to get this out properly for once and he knew the little tearaway couldn't bloody stop herself from opening that mouth of hers. "But I meant what I said. Not the insulting you and inferring that you would end up a miserable spinster part," he said sheepishly, and her eyes narrowed even further. "But the part about I think you would be good for the children, about how you could have a good life in Scotland with freedom and as many horses as you could want? I meant that."

He spotted some dark emotion flash through her eyes, gone as quicky as it had come.

"Give me these three weeks. Let me prove to you that we would be a good match. Let me show you how much the children would benefit from having you in their lives."

He dropped his hand to hear her answer. She hadn't slapped him yet. That should be a good sign, should it?

"Your Grace."

"Devon, please." He hated hearing her address him so formally.

She sighed, and he expected her to argue, even after the last few hours they'd just spent together.

"Devon," she conceded to his surprise. "You do realize how utterly insane this is, don't you?"

"I don't think it is," he said frankly. "There aren't many people whose company I enjoy. And there is not one woman of my acquaintance that I could imagine tolerating for the length of a marriage. Even with a property the size of Farnshire Castle between us."

Once again that odd look flittered through her eyes. "But you think you could tolerate me?"

Secretly, he thought he could do a lot more than tolerate her, but he wasn't ready to even begin to consider those emotions, and she certainly wasn't ready to hear them.

"I think we could tolerate each other," he said with a smile.

He waited, more nervous than he could ever remember being.

"Three weeks to decide?"

"Three weeks to decide."

And finally, she nodded, the action so tiny it was barely perceptible. But it was enough. For now, it was enough.

Chapter Fifteen

"**H**ELLO, HANDSOME. I'M so glad to see you this morning. Look how wonderful you look in the morning sun."

"So, one really *does* need to be a horse to get a compliment from you?"

Sophia froze at the sound of Devon's voice behind her, but she didn't turn away from Aengus. She couldn't until she was sure she wouldn't do something foolish like throw herself at him.

Last night had been, well, it had been so monumental that she'd gotten out of her bed this morning and run to the stables before anyone else had even stirred. It wasn't that she was afraid to face him or face up to what she'd agreed to. And it wasn't that she was terrified Francesca would take one look at her and know she'd been up to something less than proper with the duke. She just wanted some peace and quiet. That's what she'd told herself, and she'd even started to believe it. Right up until this second.

"Good morning, Your Grace," she mumbled to the horse and not the man.

"Your Grace?"

He'd stepped closer. She knew because his scent hit her at the same time as that low voice growled in her ear.

"Haven't we moved past that?"

Oh Lord. This was crazy. Just the sound of his made her excited. "I suppose we have," she muttered, still refusing to turn around.

"Is there something particularly fascinating on Aengus's flank, Sophia? Or are you just afraid to look at me?"

She knew he was baiting her, and she cursed herself for letting it work even as she spun around to glare up at him. The grin on his face said he knew exactly what he was doing, too, and she opened her mouth to ring a peal over his head. But before she got the chance to, he beat her to it. "Good morning, lass," he said, reaching out and pushing an errant curl back from her face.

Sophia felt her cheeks heat at the touch of his hand. At the soft tenderness in his voice. But then she quickly reminded herself that it didn't mean anything. Just as she'd had to remind herself of the same thing when she'd hurried back to her bedchamber last night. She couldn't and wouldn't deny the fire between them. But he'd made no secret of the fact that what he wanted from her was a business arrangement. A marriage based on convenience for him, a mother figure for the children he didn't really understand, and a chance to be a wealthy duchess for her, even though that wasn't important to her.

Agreeing to even consider it had been a huge mistake, and she needed to tell him so. But his hand was still on her neck, his thumb rubbing against her cheek, and she couldn't seem to bring herself to say the words.

The attraction between them, that heat that crackled through her veins was a constant now. And she saw no reason not to enjoy it since she had never really planned to marry in any case, so it wasn't as though she were ruining a reputation she cared a jot about.

It was just that she never thought she'd even begin to consider something so cynical, so devoid of emotion. She wasn't a bleeding heart like Elodie or a hopeless romantic like Hope. And she was well aware that most *ton* marriages were more business arrangement than anything else.

Her sisters had all found true, undeniable love, but that was the rarest of things. It stood to reason that they wouldn't *all* do so. And she'd never really been interested in anyone, so it wasn't as though she'd be missing out...

Deciding that the tiny ache in her heart was best ignored and not examined too closely, she pasted a bright smile on her face. "It's a little early for skating," she said for want of anything else to break the odd tension floating between them.

He studied her face for an age, staring so deeply into her eyes that she found herself wondering what he was looking for. But then that oddly intense expression cleared, and he dropped his hand, the roguish grin firmly back in place.

"So it is," he agreed. "But not too early for a morning ride? I assume you were about to kidnap my horse?"

She should probably be ashamed at being caught red-handed, but she didn't particularly care, so she shrugged. "I prefer to think of it as doing you the favor of exercising Aengus while you're otherwise engaged."

"Ah," he said, nodding. "But then, I'm not currently otherwise engaged, am I?"

Sophia narrowed her eyes at him. She really did want to take his stallion out. Adam's horses were beautiful, and she had one of her own at the manor for when she'd need to eventually show her face at Mama's, but she'd never ridden a horse as powerful as Aengus, and she'd been looking forward to the thrill of a gallop through the frosty countryside.

"But, you..."

He folded his arms, and she worked not to be preoccupied by the way his muscles bulged. He was ridiculously oversized. It was terribly distracting. Raising an infuriating brow, he merely stood and waited her out.

Finally, with a sigh of defeat, she folded her own arms. "Fine. What do you want?"

"I beg your pardon?"

"To let me borrow—"

"You mean kidnap."

"I mean *borrow* your horse. What do you want?"

His expression became positively wolfish, and Sophia had to

dig her riding boots into the stable floor to keep from taking a step back. "That is a very dangerous question, lass. I can think of many, many things I want from you."

Sophia's breath caught as his words sent a dart of desire straight to the core of her. He was dangerous. Incredibly, deliciously, wickedly dangerous. And this time she did take a step back as he began inching toward her.

"But sadly, what I really want isn't really suitable for a stable in the depths of winter," he drawled, coming to a stop when her back hit the wall and he was mere inches from her, towering over her and overwhelming her with his scent and heat and just—him. "So I'll settle for an invitation to join you." He paused. "And a kiss to seal the deal."

She opened her mouth to tell him what he could do with his deal, but he reached out and clasped the nape of her neck. And by the time his mouth captured her own, she'd already capitulated.

He kissed her until her breathing was ragged, until her heart felt as though it would thump straight out of her chest, until she couldn't remember what she'd been about to object to, until she could barely remember her own name.

Stepping back from her, he drew an unsteady breath and shook his head. "Let's get out of here," he said, his tone gruff and coarse. "Before I decide that a stable floor is perfectly suitable."

And because she didn't trust herself to speak at that particular moment, Sophia let him lift her onto Aengus's back, watching mutely as he blatantly stole Ares from his stall and then preceded her out of the stables and into the cold winter morning.

DEVON COULDN'T SEEM to keep the smile from his face as he and Sophia raced over Adam's grounds and into the countryside surrounding them. He had pulled back a little to let her lead the way, ostensibly because she knew the area better but really, he'd needed to take a second to gather himself.

Having spent the rest of his night tossing and turning, his body aching for Sophia, he'd awoken this morning and immediately set out for the stables, guessing that she might have had trouble sleeping and that she'd probably be there. And he'd been right, too.

He'd watched her for a moment, watched the morning sunlight dance over her chestnut locks, highlighting strands of deep, sinful red. Aengus was like a docile puppy, whinnying happily as she stroked his flank and murmured to him. His proud, strong, brutal warhorse brought to heel with just a smile from her.

He knew the feeling.

They reined in at the top of a country lane, a modest but well-situated stone farmhouse visible in the distance. Devon was desperate to make sure she hadn't changed her mind about him, about giving him a chance. But he didn't like how important it felt to him, so he stayed quiet until he could get his confusing, terrifying thoughts in order.

Sophia Templeworth was one of the most stubborn women he'd ever met in his life. Winning even the chance to bring her around to his way of thinking had been hard enough. He couldn't go changing things now. He couldn't start believing romantic notions about feelings and love. That way led problems. And he had problems enough as it was.

She turned to look at him, grinning from the thrill of the ride, her cheeks flushed from the cold wind that had whipped her hair from her face as she'd given Aengus his head. She was an incredible horsewoman. And he felt a surge of something that felt strangely like pride as he took in the sight of her in the saddle.

She didn't stay in the saddle for long, however, swinging her leg over and nearly giving him an apoplexy as she jumped from Aengus's back. He hurried to dismount in case she stumbled from the drop, but of course, she landed on her feet like a cat.

"You should wait for me to assist you," he grumbled and she eyed him.

"Why would I do that?"

"Because you could have hurt yourself."

She rolled her eyes and turned away from him to gather up Aengus's reins. "I've been dismounting horses long before I met you, Your Grace. I didn't need your help when I was in short skirts, and I don't need it now."

He scowled at her but decided this particular hill wasn't worth dying on, so he cast his gaze around the area. "Any reason we've stopped here?"

"This is the Harrison farm," she said, sounding less than pleased about it. "We need to walk the horses down this lane and open the gate at the other side to cut through it. The trees hang too low to stay on horseback. Especially for someone as big as you."

He smirked at the flush that stained her cheeks while she ran her eyes over him. He must look like a giant to her, he thought, given that she only came up to his chest. "And you have a problem with walking?" he asked.

Her sigh sounded as though it came from the depths of her soul. "No," she said sourly. "I have a problem with Philip Harrison. The pig farmer."

For a moment, Devon had no idea who she could mean. And then it dawned on him. The pig farmer who'd first wanted her sisters and now had set his sights on her. A sickening feeling suspiciously like jealousy reared its head inside him, but Devon ignored it.

It was ridiculous for a duke to be envious of a pig farmer, he told himself haughtily. Besides, there was a high likelihood that they wouldn't even come across the man on their little shortcut.

"I think…"

"Miss Templeworth! Miss Templeworth!"

Whatever Devon had been about to say was drowned out by the arrival of a rotund, shouting man.

The language Sophia used would have been at home by the docks, and he couldn't help laughing at her look of disgust.

"The pig farmer, I presume?" he asked, earning himself a scowl that could curdle milk.

By now, the man had reached them, and Devon peered down at him as he leaned over gulping gasps of air, sweat dripping from his brow. "Miss Sophia, what a delightful coincidence. I was just on my way to see you."

Devon watched as the man's greedy little eyes raked over Sophia's fitted jacket and breeches, and he found himself grinding his jaw in anger.

"Why on earth would you do that?" she demanded, and Devon smirked as the farmer's jaw dropped.

"Oh, well. I—your mother, a—that is to say, I thought that perhaps you might consent to taking a walk with me," he stuttered like a damned idiot, reaching into his pocket for a handkerchief to mop his brow.

His eyes darted to Devon and back again, clearly awaiting an introduction. Sophia, unsurprisingly, did no such thing. Her chin lifted in that tell-tale way of hers, and Devon almost felt sorry for the man. Almost.

"I'm afraid the lady's time is occupied," he said before she let her tongue loose.

"A-and who might you be?"

Devon had to give the man credit, it took guts to question him, even if he'd turned green and looked as though he might cast up his accounts.

"The Duke of Farnshire," he answered, enjoying how the other man paled from green to milk-white in an instance. "Who might you be?"

"Your Grace." The bow nearly took the man off his feet, but he managed to straighten himself. "I am Philip Harrison. A-a..."

"A pig farmer," Sophia offered, her voice saccharine. "Good day, Philip." She made to step around him, but Harrison sidestepped until he was back in her path. This time, Devon did nothing to temper his anger as he glowered down at the audacious man.

"Your mother mentioned that you are to attend the ball at the Assembly Rooms on Friday, Miss Templeworth. And I wondered if I might be so bold as to request the first two..."

"I'm afraid the lady's dance card is full, Mr. Harrison," Devon interrupted smoothly just like he had moments ago. This time, though, he felt Sophia's eyes throwing daggers at him, so he kept his own trained on the pig farmer.

The smaller man seemed to hesitate, and Devon wondered if he'd have the nerve to argue, but after only a second or two, he saw the resignation settle over his slumped shoulders. He bid them a miserable sounding farewell, then turned and wandered dejectedly back the way he'd come.

Devon steeled himself for Sophia's ire as he turned toward her. And damned if he didn't flinch, just a little bit, at the venom in her gaze.

"We should get back," he said carefully. "The children will be waiting for us to skate."

She didn't say anything, but he could feel her irritation coming off her in waves. Wordlessly, she turned and mounted Aengus with expert ease, pulling her entire body weight up on one stirrup. It probably shouldn't have made his cock twitch, but he was coming to learn he had absolutely no self-control over this woman.

As they rode back in the direction of Heywood Manor, he tried breaking the ice again. "At least I saved you from having to dance with the pig farmer," he ventured.

"Shut up, Devon," she bit out.

So, he did.

Chapter Sixteen

"**U**NCLE DEVON! LOOK at this."
Sophia laughed as she watched Finn glide over the glassy surface of the pond, attempting a spin and then falling over on his rear end. Heather's laughter rang out through the afternoon, joined seconds later by Finn's.

She watched surprise then relief flash across Devon's face at the sound of the boy's giggle and realized that he must not have heard it in a long time, if ever, and her heart fluttered in response.

"Sophia Templeworth, I never thought I'd see the day."

Sophia turned to see Cheska grinning at her and immediately her hackles went up. "What?" she snapped.

"Oh nothing. It's just that here you sit making moon eyes at the duke, and he only has two legs. I counted."

Sophia's heart hammered, but she managed to scoff, nonetheless. "What *are* you talking about?" she groused.

"Miss 'I shall never care about anything that isn't a horse' seems to have taken a shine to our devilishly handsome duke. Like I said, I never thought I'd see the day."

"I haven't taken a shine to anyone," Sophia countered grumpily, but there was no heat in it. She knew it, and Cheska knew it, too.

"There are worse things in the world than being attracted to the man who wants to marry you, Sophia," Francesca said gently.

Yes, like feeling more than just attraction for a man who sees you as a business transaction. The errant thought popped into her head before she could silence it. And it unsettled her so much that she jumped to her feet.

"I think I'll skate again," she said even though the only reason she was sitting here beside Francesca wrapped in a blanket was because she'd been freezing out there on the ice.

"But you haven't had your apple cider yet," Cheska argued, though Sophia was already shuffling toward the ice. Walking in skates was nearly impossible, but it was worth risking a twisted ankle or two to get away from her sister's knowing looks.

She felt a slight twinge of guilt for abandoning Francesca, but she needn't have worried, for by the time she'd stepped onto the ice, Adam was right back at Francesca's side fussing over her like a mother hen.

"Sophia, come skate." Before she knew what she was about, a tiny hand reached up and pulled her forward, stumbling face first toward the ice.

She let out an undignified screech as she tumbled toward the frozen surface, but right before she hit it, she was swept up into a pair of impossibly strong arms. Even if he hadn't been the only other person on the ice, she would have recognized them as Devon's.

"Be careful with Sophia, Heather," he said gently as he set her on her feet. And though he addressed the little girl who was now watching them wide-eyed, he kept his gaze trained on her. "We can't have anything happening to that beautiful face, can we?"

"No, Uncle Devon," the little girl said dutifully.

"Shall we?" He held out his arm as though he were about to escort her through the most prestigious of ballrooms, and she laughed as she took it.

As they set off, she felt a tug on her cloak and looked down to see Heather gripping it, smiling up her. Finn came flying toward them, skidding to a stop right at Devon's side before setting off with them, chattering away to his uncle about whether or not he'd be able to jump and land on his feet. And as they skated,

Sophia felt an overwhelming happiness course through her veins. A sense of home, though that was madness of course.

But try as she might, she couldn't quite shake the feeling, and as they skated by where Adam had Francesca wrapped tightly in his arms, holding her hand as though it was the most precious jewel in Christendom, she couldn't help but think how wonderful it felt to have someone's hand holding onto her, too.

So, when Francesca raised a brow, and Sophia stuck her tongue out childishly in response, she couldn't even get angry about the look on Francesca's face that said she didn't believe Sophia's denials about wanting this for herself. Because the truth was, she wasn't sure she believed it herself.

THE ASSEMBLY ROOMS in Halton were much like Assembly Rooms in every other small town or village he'd been in. Though there was definitely something odd about this place and the people in it.

He was used to a certain amount of fawning, of course. It came with the territory of being a duke, though it had been in short supply at Heywood Manor. Adam, being a marquess himself, and one of Devon's oldest friends, didn't give a damn about his own title, let alone Devon's. And the Templeworth misses didn't give a damn about anything, really. Perhaps a little fawning would do his ego some good.

He cast an eye around the room ostensibly to take in his surroundings, but he was looking for her. Strange as it was, he felt as though he *missed* her. Since their afternoon skating on the pond the other day, he'd barely let her out of his sight. He was determined to get a yes from her before he needed to return to Scotland, and so he'd spent the last few days with her and the children trying his damnedest to show her what a good life they could have.

Only, only it was starting to feel less like showing off a good arrangement and more like just enjoying her company. And he wasn't sure what that meant or quite what to do with it.

He hadn't had the chance to kiss her or touch her properly in days, and that was eating him alive, too. That must be why it felt as though he was aching for her. Lust, pure and simple. She was a beautiful woman, and now that he knew how she felt, how she tasted, how she came apart in his arms, he craved more of it. Any red-blooded man would. It was perfectly normal.

Looking around again, he smiled and nodded at the various greetings and smiles being sent his way. She still wasn't here, and since he'd maneuvered himself into dancing with her, he wanted her to hurry up and get here. Wanted the excuse of a dance to hold her again, even if it was only for seconds in a room full of people.

She'd been summoned home this morning by a letter that had arrived from her mother. Ironic since she and her sister had just been discussing how odd it was that the woman hadn't arrived to throw herself at Devon's feet already. As soon as she'd opened her letter, her eyes had narrowed, and Devon found himself wondering if he should get the children out of the line of fire. They no longer ate their morning meal in the nursery. Instead, Sophia sent him to collect them and bring them down to join the adults. And he, like a damned lady's maid, ran to do her bidding.

And yet, he found that he enjoyed every second of it. Immensely. The children had come alive under Sophia's attention and, yes, his own. Finn was smiling more, laughing even. He'd come so far in just over a week of being here. Originally, he'd proposed this arrangement because he thought he could leave the children in her hands and they'd be happy and loved and taken care of. But of course, her being who she was, she'd flipped his plan on its head and somehow bridged the gap between he and his wards.

The only time he'd regretted having the children take their

meals with them had been when she'd gotten that missive from her mother, demanding she return home and explain her encounter with the pig farmer. Heather and Finn had heard words then that he'd rather weren't in their vocabulary. But before he'd even been able to question her about it, she'd mumbled something about Mrs. Templeworth threatening to come for a visit and had swept out of the room. He hadn't seen her since. In fact, he didn't even know if she'd show up tonight.

"You really are living up to that intimidating duke reputation, Devon. You're scaring the locals." Devon turned to see Adam hold out a goblet to him. He took it, scowling at the contents. He'd prefer brandy, as would Adam, he knew.

"If they could survive your wounded soldier phase, they can survive my not feeling very festive," he countered with a raised brow. He still marveled at the change in his friend from the haunted shell of a person he was before he'd come back to Halton. Although, now that he'd met in indomitable Templeworth women, he wasn't as surprised. He knew firsthand now what a difference that made.

"Fair enough," Adam laughed. "But you're not usually so brooding. What's wrong with you?"

Devon knew better than to say that his mood had anything to do with Sophia. He'd only just managed to smooth things over when Adam had caught them outside the nursery last week. To admit that he was standing here pining for her, that he was desperate to get his hands on her again would be akin to a death wish. The only reason they hadn't already come to blows was that Devon had been completely honest with his old friend. Had told him the complete truth. Had explained that he wanted Sophia for his duchess, on a strictly platonic, logical basis, and that she'd deigned to give him the scraps of these few, short weeks to convince her to agree. Adam had found the whole thing hilarious. Devon had not.

But now it didn't feel as though that *was* the complete truth, and he didn't know how to explain that to himself let alone her overprotective brother-in-law.

"Nothing," he lied smoothly. "Just taking it all in." He could feel Adam's eyes boring into him, so he kept his own purposely trained on the townsfolk milling around.

"Because it's all so riveting?" Adam asked drily, and Devon knew that Adam knew that he was talking horseshit.

Before he could scramble to say something appeasing however, the marchioness, who'd been accosted the moment they'd walked in the door, broke away from the gaggle of ladies she'd been talking to and smiled over at her husband. Devon could practically feel Adam lose interest in their conversation. Without a word of farewell, he walked straight over to his wife, ignoring everyone and everything but her.

And Devon felt a lance of jealousy that Adam could do so. Freely and without worrying about propriety or confusing feelings. He wasn't confused. He blatantly and unapologetically loved his wife, and she loved him back, fiercely. It wasn't something he'd ever cared about before, but now? Now he was starting to suspect that he might care a great deal.

A commotion at the door signaled a new arrival, and Devon looked up to see Sophia arrive with whom, he assumed, was her mother. His eyes raked over her from that hair, pulled and pinned into submission, to the snow-white gown that made her look like an angel, and straight back to those eyes that had kept him awake and longing every single night.

He kept his gaze on her face and choked out an answer, nonetheless.

"Riveting."

Chapter Seventeen

"D R. PEARSE, I'VE been trying my hardest to think of a polite way to say this, but honestly, I'm running out of patience, so I have to be honest. I don't care about your great-aunt's dog's broken leg. I understand that I probably should, and that it's quite rude to tell you so, and that it probably makes me a terrible person, but there you have it."

Sophia registered the shock on the doctor's plain but pleasant enough face. She heard her mother's gasped "oh no" before the groan that said once again, my daughter has disappointed me. But she couldn't quite bring herself to care about either of them. Not when she could feel Devon's eyes on her from across the room. Not when she'd spent the entire day listening to Mama. First it had been the interrogation about whether the duke had any intentions toward her. Then the caterwauling when Sophia had smoothly lied and said that the duke was affianced.

It wouldn't be a lie if she agreed to marry him, of course. But hell itself would freeze over before Sophia told her grasping mother that a *duke* was available and staying under the same roof as she.

Of course the hysteria soon gave way to the real reason she'd been summoned, and the rest of the afternoon had been spent listening to sermon after sermon about how rude she'd been to the pig farmer, how she shouldn't dance with the duke or anyone else unless there was a marriage to be made at the end of the cotillion, and how Mr. Harrison's mama had graciously agreed to let Sophia make it up to her odious son.

And when Sophia had rightly pointed out that it was pathetic that he'd gone running to his mother to tell tales, she'd endured *another* lecture about the embarrassment of being a spinster when all her sisters had caught themselves peers of the realm. It had been so tempting to bite back. To tell her mother that she could be a *duchess* if she wanted to be. If she weren't so foolish as to want something as ridiculous as love, she could have a peer of her own.

But that wasn't a battle worth fighting. She was dealing with enough of her own emotions. She wasn't bloody well taking on her mother's, too. The silence was growing deafening, and she was about to just turn on her heels and walk away when another voice sounded behind her.

"Miss Templeworth, I believe the dancing is about to start."

She looked around and then up into Devon's face, a little panicked by the flutter of joy at the sight of him. The butterflies, she thought with an internal grimace. She wasn't exactly pleased about how much she'd missed him today. Nor was she pleased about what being so close to him was doing to her.

Before she could respond, however, the banal doctor got there before her. "Yes, I was going to ask, Miss Templeworth, if you would do me the honor of..."

"Shall we?"

Devon's voice cut across Dr. Pearse's as though the man hadn't even spoken, and Sophia couldn't contain her grin even though a part of her was annoyed by his high-handedness. But she'd infinitely rather dance with him than listen to any more of the dull doctor's anecdotes.

"I didn't realize this dance was taken." Well, Dr. Pearse was persistent, she'd give him that. "Perhaps the next."

"That dance is taken, too," Devon interrupted, claiming her hand just as he had with Philip Harrison. And though she didn't have a jot of interest in dancing with either of those men, her annoyance grew ten-fold.

"Actually, I don't intend to dance tonight at all," she said with faux sweetness, ignoring the thumping of her heart in response to the duke's raised brow.

"Sophia, won't you introduce me to your friend?"

Sophia had to grit her teeth to stop from saying something rude in answer to Mama's obsequiousness. She knew very well who Devon was, as was evidenced by the fact that she was practically genuflecting at his feet. "I don't know," she said with a shrug. "I've never met him, he just keeps following me around."

She didn't know whose reaction she enjoyed most. Dr. Pearse's shock, Devon's scowl of displeasure, or Mama's horrified gasp followed by yet another groan of defeat. Probably all three.

"Now, if you'll all excuse me?" She made to walk away, but Devon still had hold of her hand and he swiftly pulled her to a firm if gentle stop.

He bent down to whisper in her ear, and she couldn't contain her tremble as a *frisson* of awareness spiked through her. "Introduce me to your mother, lass," he said in a tone that brooked no argument, and while she would usually rebel against such high-handedness, she found herself quite inexplicably doing as she was told.

Rolling her eyes at him she turned back to face Mama and Dr. Pearse, who still hadn't had the sense to just slink off somewhere else. "Mama, allow me to introduce His Grace, the Duke of Farnshire. Your Grace, my mother Mrs. Templeworth." Mama curtsied so low, she was practically prostrate, and Sophia rolled her eyes again. "And Dr. Pearse," she said with a wave of her hand in his general direction.

"Your Grace," Mama said, her tone nasally and weirdly high pitched, "I cannot tell you what an honor it is to have you here in our little village. I so look forward to enjoying Christmas with you."

Devon was all politeness as he bowed to Mama, then patient-ly listened to her rabbiting on, throwing embarrassing compliments his way and generally just fawning and carrying on ridiculously.

And Sophia really did her best to sneak away more than once but that damned, giant paw of his kept hold of her wrist, refusing to let her go.

The opening strands of a quadrille sounded from the band of musicians in the corner, and Devon smoothly interrupted Mama's terribly nosy questions about his properties and holdings. "If you'll excuse me, Mrs. Templeworth, I promised your daughter that I would dance the first with her. She begged so much, I would feel just terrible if I didn't comply."

"Oh, but didn't you say you didn't care to dance, Miss Templeworth?"

Before Sophia could respond, Devon bowed to her mother, ignored Dr. Perse, and practically dragged her toward where the other dancers had already congregated. "I *begged* you to dance with me?" she hissed through clenched teeth as he placed her beside the ladies before moving to stand in line with the gentlemen.

"Yes," he hissed right back. "Right around the time I was following you around without you knowing who I was."

Ah, so that was payback for her little joke. The dance began, and they walked toward each other, Sophia having to crane her neck to scowl up at him. "Do you have any idea what you've done?" She quickly dropped into a curtsy half a second after the other ladies. "The ideas she'll get now that you've made her think I've been begging for your attention?"

They stepped back away from each other again as the dance required, and she had to wait for what felt like an age until they moved together again and clasped hands.

"If memory serves, I *did* have you begging for my attention," he whispered with a knowing smirk, the heat in his eyes telling her exactly what he was referring to, and to her utmost annoyance, she felt her cheeks redden in response.

"I should have left you with my mother," she sniped back.

"You could have had your ego well and truly fed by her salivating over the size of your *holding*." She paused a second before continuing, her voice sickly sweet. "I would have enjoyed telling her how unimpressive it really is."

It was his turn to scowl, and Sophia couldn't contain her smug grin as she got one up on him.

"You are a little brat," he said through his teeth as they promenaded between the line of dancers before taking their place at the end.

"And you are an overbearing oaf," she snapped. "What are you about, telling everyone I'm not dancing with them?"

"Did you *want* to dance with that sniveling little doctor or your precious pig farmer?" he countered, his eyes flashing.

"Of course, I didn't," she practically screeched, drawing more than one glance for the townsfolk surrounding them. "But I don't need you swooping in to the rescue every time someone talks to me. I am perfectly capable of handling these things myself."

The dance by now was quite forgotten. They were just two people arguing in the middle of a countryside Assembly Room. The idiocy of the moment wasn't lost on her.

"I didn't do it because I think you're incapable of handling a couple of little rodents, Sophia," he growled, stomping forward until he was towering over her.

"Then why did you do it?" she demanded, refusing to be intimidated. And especially refusing to be distracted by his sandalwood scent.

"Because I can't stand the idea of another man's hands on you, that's why," he finally snapped. "Even if it's just for a dance."

DEVON KNEW HE'D crossed a line having this conversation in front of Sophia's family and friends. She was the most stubborn little miss in the world, but she was also the most prideful. He should have known his high-handedness would rile her. He *had* known. He just hadn't been able to help it.

As the privileged only son of a powerful duke, the heir to one of the wealthiest duchies in the realm, he'd never really had cause to experience jealousy before. But that's what it was, he realized. White-hot jealousy.

He'd watched how the doctor had salivated over her. Seen the determination in his beady little eyes and known that he would not stop pursuing her. But he should have also known that Sophia Templeworth would have died before giving in to pressure from anyone, least of all a man. Maybe he deserved her ire, but her little quip about not knowing him had hit its mark, even though it shouldn't have.

And now here he was, bellowing at her in the middle of a country dance.

"Are you two putting on some sort of play for Christmas? How marvelously entertaining." Devon turned to see Lady Heywood grinning up at them, though there was a watchfulness in her eyes at odds with the light expression.

He turned back in time to see Sophia glare at her sister. It looked as though they were silently communicating. Arguing, really. And he couldn't tell which one of them was winning.

All round them, people were whispering and staring and, Christ, here came her mother. He didn't think he had it in him to put up with that woman again, so he made a decision that was likely to land him in even more trouble.

"Lady Heywood, your sister is feeling a little under the weather. I'm going to take her home." He could hear Sophia's gasp of outrage but kept his gaze firmly away from her.

"I'm *not* under the…"

"You do look a little flushed, Sophia. Perhaps it would be better to go home. Take the carriage, Your Grace. You can return it when you get her home."

Devon tried not to let his smugness show as he nodded his thanks to the marchioness. "I'll fetch your cloak, Miss Templeworth and call for the carriage."

Before he'd taken even five steps, he heard Sophia's blistering hisses. "What the hell are you doing, Cheska? Is this revenge for telling Mama that your favorite pastime is taking tea with her and discussing how you might be better behaved? Because that was *months* ago, and you already got me back."

He didn't hear her sister's response, but his lips twitched in spite of the discord currently brewing between them. He could well imagine her tricking her sister just for the hell of it. He made a mental note to ask how Lady Heywood had paid her back. When she wasn't as angry with him of course.

It was the work of a moment to send for the carriage and fetch Sophia's cloak. As soon as he picked it up, her maddening floral scent assailed him, and like a damned idiot, he buried his nose in the material and inhaled it as deeply into his lungs as he could.

The distinctive sound of trundling carriage wheels thankfully snapped him out of it, and he hurried back into the ballroom to face the wrath of his hopefully soon-to-be-wife. Scanning the room, he saw that Adam had been accosted by his mother-in-law, and he chuckled softly to himself. The glazed look in Adam's eyes along with the tightness around his mouth was a sure sign that he was being bothered by the woman.

"Adam is keeping my mother occupied while you slip out." The marchioness appeared in front of him, a scowling Sophia firmly in her grasp. "And whilst she usually loves to have him anywhere near her, she can sense fresh meat from a mile away. So I suggest you make your escape now."

She held Sophia's arm up, and he immediately grasped her hand, tugging her along a lot more gently than her sister had handled her.

"I'm only leaving with you now because I don't want to listen to my mother," she said as she stomped along beside him.

And Devon couldn't keep the smile from his face, even though he knew it would annoy her more. "I don't care, lass," he answered truthfully. "As long as you're leaving with me."

Chapter Eighteen

S OPHIA KEPT HER eyes fixed to the window of the carriage even though it was too dark to see anything. Francesca's words were rattling around in her head, repeating over and over again until she thought she'd scream.

When she'd demanded to know why Francesca seemed to be determined to work against her, Francesca had given her a look that was almost pitying.

"I always knew it would take someone incredibly strong to match you, Sophia. To make you fall. And as much as you want to deny it, I can see what you're not yet ready to. So go with him, or I'll set the pig farmer on you."

Sophia had simply turned and walked away. And now she sat here pondering Cheska's words and wondering what they could mean. Worse still, she knew that if she looked deep enough inside of herself, she'd know exactly what her sister had meant. And that just made her angrier.

"Sophia."

Devon's voice sounded low and smooth across the small space between them, and she couldn't stop her body from reacting to it so that was another mark against him in her book. Irrational, maybe, but she wasn't feeling terribly rational.

In short, she didn't like the control he seemed to have over her. It made her feel as though she wasn't truly in charge of her own life. And she *hated* feeling like she had to cede control to anyone for any reason.

"Sophia."

Childishly, she turned her face further away from him until she was worried she'd snap her neck. His quiet laugh sounded seconds before he suddenly appeared on the bench beside her. He was so massive that she was immediately squashed between the side of the carriage and his thigh, and she whipped her head around to glare at him. "What are you doing, you great big oaf?" she snapped. "There isn't enough room for us both to sit here."

"Well, that's easily fixed," he said lightly before plucking her from her seat and placing her firmly in his lap.

The second she made contact with his body it felt as though she'd been set alight, and she squirmed against his impossibly strong hold. "Unless you want me to kiss the temper out of you, lass, you'll stop moving like that on me."

She scowled at him even as his words sent a bolt of lightning straight to her core, and she froze, feeling the evidence of what he was referring to pressing against her. And all at once all the anger, all the outrage and irritation about how he'd run roughshod over her back at the Assembly Rooms seemed to melt away in the heat of his stare.

There wasn't a sound in the carriage as Devon held her gaze. He reached out, clasped the nape of her neck, rubbing a thumb along her cheek. "You are incredibly beautiful when you're spitting mad," he said.

"And you're incredibly bossy when you're jealous," she said right back, though even she could hear there was no bite in her tone.

"Would it help if I said I was sorry?" he asked.

"That depends. Would you mean it?"

"No."

She wanted to stay angry, but his self-deprecating little smile was doing terribly distracting things to her insides.

"I didn't mean to upset you," he continued, and she really was trying not to be charmed by him. But he had dimples for goodness's sake, and she was only human. "And I know you can take care of yourself no matter who or what you face. You're just…" He hesitated, seeming to struggle with his words, and for some reason, her heart stuttered while she waited for him to speak again. Finally, he sighed and shrugged. "You're important."

Sophia refused to acknowledge the tiny twinge of disappointment she felt at his words. Surely, she couldn't have expected him to say anything else. Surely, she didn't want him to? Before she could settle her confusion though, his lips dropped to hers. The kiss was soft, tender, and swift. And he pulled back a couple of inches to stare into her eyes.

"Am I forgiven?" he whispered.

"No," she insisted, but she pressed her mouth against his again, nonetheless.

⫸⫷

DEVON WASTED NO time in deepening their kiss, plunging his tongue inside her mouth, unbale to stifle a groan at the taste of her. Her own little sounds of pleasure shot straight to his cock, and he couldn't stop himself from surging against her.

He nearly exploded right then and there when she reacted to the contact by wriggling her hips until he was pressed against her center.

Hanging onto his self-control with Herculean effort, he tried to cool things down. He really did. But then she whispered his name, the breathless sound vibrating against his lips and, well, a man only had so much restraint.

With a growl of desperation, he plunged his hand into her hair, gripping the locks to pull her head back so he could press kisses along her neck. Running his nose along the smooth skin of her jaw, he bit lightly at her earlobe, delighting in her gasp of pleasure.

Her hair came undone, spilling onto his hand and sending a

wave of that uniquely Sophia scent his way.

Christ, he couldn't get enough of her. That passion that rose to the surface at the merest of touches, the natural seductiveness that she didn't even seem to realize she possessed. She was becoming something of an obsession for him, and he didn't give a damn. Not if it meant he could keep doing this.

He ran his hand slowly down every curve of her body, a blaze trailing through his veins as he went. It wasn't enough. It was nowhere near enough.

With a muffled oath, he reached down and pulled at her skirts, desperate to get them out of his way. He needed to touch her, to feel her come apart for him again, to hear the sounds she made when he brought her to the height of pleasure.

Feeling the material of her silk stockings, he captured her mouth again as his fingers moved further and further up her leg until he finally found what he wanted—hot, satin-smooth skin, bared to his touch.

"Open for me, lass," he instructed her, growling his approval that she was actually doing as she was told. He moved his hand to cup her mound and...

The carriage came to a sudden stop, the driver's shout penetrating the fog of lust that had surrounded Devon the second he'd gotten into the damned thing, and he felt Sophia freeze in his hands before her eyes snapped open, glazed with passion but widening with horror. She must have realized, just as he did, that the door was likely to open any second.

And anyone who saw her, hair tousled and running down her back, lips swollen from his kisses, cheeks flushed and breathing labored would know immediately what they'd been doing. Not to mention the fact that walking was going to be damned impossible for him for the foreseeable future.

Before any of the panic playing about her face could set in, he lifted her and placed her on the bench across from him, leaning over to pull the hood of her cloak over her head, then sat back as though he'd been behaving himself for the entirety of their journey.

Only seconds later, the door swung open and a footman stood with an umbrella ready to escort Sophia through the falling snow. Without even looking in his direction, she scrambled from the vehicle and hurried toward the house.

Devon brushed off the second footman with an umbrella who stood by to escort him. He didn't need protection from the bloody snow. He needed Sophia. He hurried up the steps of the manor house after her. Divesting himself of his hat and greatcoat was the work of a moment, but there was still no sign of Sophia in the expansive foyer.

Cursing under his breath at the missed opportunity to spend time alone with her, he decided to drown his sorrows, smiling to himself as he went to steal some of Adam's brandy stashed in the library. He pushed open the door, hoping that he could at least get drunk enough to cool the fire still burning him up. But he stepped into the room, and there she was. She was clasping the decanter in her hands as she swung around to stare, wide-eyed, at him.

Drink quite forgotten, Devon prowled toward her. Wordlessly, he reached out and plucked the bottle from her fingers, reaching around her to place it back on the end table by the chaise.

Though he knew he was treading a dangerous path, there was no way he'd be able to walk away from her right now. Or let her go. She looked up at him, an unreadable expression in her deep brown eyes. "Did you need something?" she asked, and he could hear the attempt at bravado in her tone, but she wasn't fooling him. If the pulse racing at the base of her throat didn't give her away, the heat climbing in her cheeks would have done it.

"Yes, I need something," he said. "You." Reaching out to pull her into his arms once more. "I'm not done with you yet."

Chapter Nineteen

S OPHIA KNEW SHE should push him away. After capitulating to him so quickly, so completely in the carriage, she knew it wasn't safe to be around him. There was nothing she didn't want to give to this man. And given that she'd never wanted to give a man even the time of day before, she didn't like that she was willing to hand Devon her innocence and possibly her heart on a silver platter.

Yet, she was powerless to resist him. And she *hated* feeling powerless. The instinct to be stubborn and refuse to stay in here with him because he'd declared he wasn't done with her warred with the need throbbing through her body.

But then he reached up and took her face in his hands, his touch so gentle that her eyes smarted. "The hold you have on me is terrifying, Sophia Templeworth. I would walk over hot coals just to breathe the same air as you. How do you do it?"

She wanted to tell him that she knew the feeling. But she was still annoyed by his high-handedness so, instead, she kissed him. And the flame that had been lit in the carriage blazed all over again.

Devon's hands moved from her face to her hips, and she was hoisted into the air. She wrapped her legs around his waist, and she pulled herself closer to him while her tongue danced with his. In seconds, she was mindless. Some part of her knew they were moving, but she didn't fully comprehend it until her back made contact with the wall.

Plunging her hands into his hair, she pulled him so close that there was nothing between them. And it wasn't enough. She arched her back, and his hands were there, running along the material of her gown. The sound of material ripping rent the air, followed by the unmistakable sound of tiny, pearl buttons hitting the floor, and Sophia pulled back to stare at him in shock. "You ripped my dress," she exclaimed.

"I'll buy you a hundred dresses," he growled. "A thousand of them." And then he was kissing her again, and she didn't care about dresses or buttons or anything but him.

He pulled at the destroyed material, and she hurried to remove the sleeves until she was bared to him in only her stays and chemise. This time it was Devon who broke their kiss as he raked his eyes over her exposed flesh, the gaze so hot that she felt it burn her skin. And then his lips were there replacing the look as he kissed a trail lower and lower while those clever fingers of his found the back of her stays until it fell to the floor.

Dropping her to her feet, he stepped back until her dress pooled on the Persian rug, and she was in nothing but her chemise and stockings. He reached out and lowered the straps of her chemise with agonizing slowness until her body was covered in gooseflesh. She watched him as he stared at her body, while he untied the ribbons and let it fall.

And when she was completely naked, save for her stockings and garters, his smile became positively feral. "You are perfect," he said hoarsely.

Sophia was vaguely aware that she should probably be embarrassed and making an effort to cover herself, hide from that savage lust in his eyes. But all she felt was a need for more—more of his mouth and teeth and tongue.

He closed the inches between them again and raised her chin to drop a swift, hard kiss on her lips before moving to bite gently at her neck. "I'm going to eat you alive," he whispered into her skin. She could only grip his hair once more and hold on for dear life as he kissed his way down her body, stopping to worship first one breast and then the other.

And then, to her shock, he dropped to his knees before her, gripping her thighs and pulling them apart.

"W-what are you doing?" she stammered.

"I told you," he said, smiling up at her, his eyes glowing with unreserved lust. "I'm going to eat you alive."

And before she could ask him what he meant, his mouth went straight to the center of her need. Sophia cried out, shock and a pleasure so intense making her legs quiver, and she would have fallen if not for his impossible strong grip on her legs.

Sensation after sensation battered her as he unleashed himself. The knot of pleasure inside her twisted tighter and tighter until it was bordering on pain, and she couldn't stop her sobs, couldn't hold back her moans. And just when she thought she'd die from the tension, he plunged his finger inside her, hooking it until it hit a spot that had her bursting into a million pieces.

She cried out, the release making her knees buckle. It felt like an eternity before her breathing returned to normal. Devon pressed his head against her stomach, his own breathing seeming almost as labored as her own.

She stroked his hair, noticing that even her hands shook from the intensity of what he'd wrought in her. If she didn't know better, she would think he looked, well, that was foolish. She *did* know better. He'd made it very clear that he wanted her for convenience and nothing else. And attraction didn't mean love. She knew that.

He stood to his full height, towering over her once again. And she noticed for the first time the gaping disparity between them. He stood there still fully dressed, still looking as though he could glide into a ballroom looking every inch the immaculately turned-out duke. Nothing out of place except the hair that she'd mussed. And she stood here, completely naked.

And the self-consciousness that had been missing earlier came back with a vengeance. "I—"

The sound of Francesca and Adam laughing suddenly sounded from down the corridor, and Sophia's eyes widened in terror. "Oh, good heavens," she whispered.

Devon's language was a lot more colorful. In seconds, he'd removed his dinner jacket and thrown it over her shoulders. It swamped her and surrounded her with his scent, and it took considerable effort not to bury her nose in it.

His eyes raked over her, and he swore again under his breath. "It's very inconvenient that you look that good in my jacket," he murmured, but before she could question him, he scooped up her discarded clothing and shoved the pile into her hands. "Come," he said, gently taking her arm and pulling her toward the door. He opened it and stuck his head out looking up and down the darkened corridor, then turned back to face her.

"It's clear," he whispered. "Take the backstairs to your bedchamber. I'll keep them distracted so you can slip inside without them seeing you."

Too anxious to even speak, Sophia nodded her understanding before slipping past him and into the corridor. She'd only taken a step before his hands were on her shoulders spinning her around to face him. He pressed a brief kiss to her mouth, then turned her around again and gave her a gentle shove to get her moving.

Miraculously, Sophia made it to her chamber without seeing a single soul. She closed her door and then locked it for good measure, not wanting Cheska to check on her. She knew she wouldn't be able to keep the truth from her sister, and she didn't want to talk about it until she could at least breathe properly.

She staggered to the bed on knees that still felt shaky, throwing her gown, chemise, and stays on the floor beside it and climbing under the cover. And only when she was curled up in an exhausted ball did she allow herself to inhale the scent of Devon.

"YOU'RE BACK. I—OH."

Devon had been furiously wracking his brain to come up with an excuse to keep Adam and his wife occupied but judging by what he'd just walked into, he needn't have worried.

"Devon, go away," Adam said, keeping hold of Lady Heywood when she would have pulled back. "Can't you see I'm busy?"

"Er, yes. I'll just bid you goodnight and…"

"Where's Sophia?"

Devon's heart slammed against his ribcage which was ridiculous since it was a perfectly innocuous question that the marchioness had asked. "Hmm? Oh yes, you're sister. She—she's ah—in bed."

They both frowned, and he tried to get a hold of himself. He knew that if Adam suspected what had just gone on then he'd either shoot him or try to force Sophia to marry him. And knowing her the way he did, he knew which option would win out.

Besides, even though he'd gone into this wanting a formal, logical, *sensible,* and emotionless marriage, he found that he didn't want Sophia's hand forced even if it meant him ultimately getting his way. Because he knew deep down, he didn't want it like that. He wanted Sophia to *want* it. To have choices before her and to pick him.

It was probably too big as ask but he couldn't control how he felt, and he was getting very close to being done fighting it.

"You didn't get up to anything scandalous, did you?" Francesca asked, putting the fear of God into him.

"Not at all," he lied as smoothly as possible. "She had a headache, so she went straight upstairs as soon as we got home."

"Really?" the marchioness asked, her eyes narrowing suspiciously, and he resisted the urge to loosen his cravat.

"Really," he confirmed.

"Oh. How terribly disappointing," she said with a shrug. Damned if she wasn't as outrageous as her sister. Her sister who only moments ago had been standing before him completely naked. He almost groaned aloud at the memory. He'd never seen anyone so exquisite. He'd damn near lost his mind trying to decide where to touch first, where to taste.

"Devon?"

Realizing that Adam had been trying to get his attention, Devon attempted to school his features into a mask of polite indifference. He had no idea if it was working or not. He kept perfectly still trying not to fidget while Francesca reached up to whisper something in Adam's ear.

Adam's eyes darted from his wife to Devon and back again before he nodded and dropped a kiss on her brow.

With a raised brow and a quick wave, she swept from the room leaving them alone. There was a moment of stilted silence before Adam sighed. "Drink?" he asked, an edge to his voice but one Devon couldn't quite judge. And since he knew he wouldn't get a wink of sleep now that he'd seen Sophia naked and writhing under his touch, he figured he might as well get drunk with one of his oldest friends.

Chapter Twenty

"THERE YOU ARE. How are you feeling, dear?" Sophia smiled at Cheska's greeting but her eyes were drawn straight to Devon who'd jumped to his feet the second she'd entered the room.

"Sophia?"

"Oh, um. Yes. Yes, I'm well. Where are the children?" Usually, Heather and Finn insisted on sitting either side of her and would have acted as a buffer this morning. But there was no sign of them, and she was terrified that she'd give herself away without their presence. That something in her face would tell Francesca or even Adam that a line had been crossed last night.

"His Grace mentioned you were ill last night, so I thought it prudent to keep things a little quieter this morning," Francesca answered smoothly. "I sent them to harass Severin by telling them he had gingerbread in his pockets. From the screeches I think they followed him to the kitchens."

Sophia laughed despite her uneasiness. Adam's cook had German relatives and she made the most delicious yuletide treats from family recipes that she swore she would take to the grave. Sophia tormented her so much that she'd taken to just having a constant supply.

"Won't you sit, Miss Templeworth?" Devon's voice was so gentle as he pulled out the chair by his that it made her stomach clench, but she kept her face politely bland as she sat, aware of

Francesca's and Adam's eyes on her.

"Are you feeling better, Sophia?" She snapped her eyes to Adam at his question. He was staring intently at her, and she couldn't help but feel as though she were in some sort of trouble.

"Er, yes thank you."

"That's good to hear."

There was a stilted pause and Sophia began to think that she'd missed something important. She'd been awake last night when Francesca had come knocking at her door, but she'd ignored her sister in favor of tossing and turning alone all night wondering if Devon had let anything slip, then wondering how he felt about what had happened, then wondering if her body would ever stop aching for him. It had been exhausting and infuriating in equal measure.

"And what was it that you said was wrong?"

"A stomachache," she said swiftly which would have been fine if Devon hadn't answered at the exact same moment.

"A headache."

This time the silence was deafening, and she sat frozen while Adam glared at her and Devon, and Francesca snorted into her tea.

"Honestly, Sophia. If you're going to lie about what you've been up to you should have least have your stories straight. I'm disappointed in you, you know better than that."

"Sweetheart, that's not helpful."

"Yes, but that's my point. She's no amateur, she shouldn't *need* help."

Adam and Francesca bickered back and forth for a time while Sophia just sat there trying to sort through her feelings. It had occurred to her in the night that Adam had only allowed Devon to take her home from the dance because he knew Devon was planning on her accepting her proposal.

And as the sun had risen over the frost-tipped grounds, she had to finally face her feelings. Finally stop fighting her heart and accept the truth. So, she had stripped away all of her stubbornness, all of her determination to be the mistress of her own fate. And with that thought, that final piece of the puzzle fell into place, and the picture became blindingly, frighteningly clear; she'd fallen in love with the duke. The love her sisters had for their husbands. The love she'd mocked them all for. The loved she'd sworn she was incapable of feeling. It had happened to her. Despite her best efforts to only ever care for something with four legs, she'd been brought down by this man.

And somehow, that made things worse. Because if she accepted his proposal, she would have to accept that she would spend her life loving a man who only wanted her for convenience. Yes, he might be attracted to her, he might even like her sometimes, though she doubted it. But love? He'd made it brutally clear that love wasn't a part of this deal and never would be.

Plus, she knew her mother would be ecstatic beyond words if she were to marry a duke. If she finally gave in to his proposal, she'd have to accept that Mama would make an absolute spectacle of her for years to come.

Yet even knowing that couldn't temper her feelings. And she'd known for longer than she cared to admit that she loved him. Just as she knew he didn't love her back. So now here she was stuck in the ridiculous circumstance of getting to marry the man she adored and feeling utterly miserable about it.

Suddenly she felt as though she was going to burst out of her skin and when Devon's hand slipped from the table to squeeze her leg, she jumped up so quickly that she rattled all the cutlery and knocked over her teacup. The action at least brough a cessation to Francesca's and Adam's bickering but it also meant that all eyes were trained on her. "I-I'm sorry," she stuttered nervously even though she'd always prided herself on never being nervous. "I just need some air. The headache, or stomachache I mean." She was growing more flustered by the second. "The headache *and* stomachache," she continued a little desperately, "are bothering me again. I'll see you all later."

"Sophia!"

"Miss Templeworth!"

The calls of Adam, Cheska, and Devon followed her out of the room, but Sophia ignored them all. She needed space. She needed to think. She needed to get away from everyone and everything until her mind stopped spinning. So, without a backward glance she ran straight out of the manor house and to the stables, her heart hammering in her chest and her eyes, rather annoyingly, filling with tears.

THE SILENCE SOPHIA left in her wake was filled with so much tension that Devon felt as though he'd be able to cut it with a knife. But regardless of what Adam or even his wife thought, his priority right now was to get to Sophia.

He had no idea why she had seemed so upset this morning, and he was terrified that if he didn't go after her right now, she'd say no to his proposal and he'd lose her from his life forever.

But he hadn't taken more than three steps towards the door before Adam was in front of him, his face like thunder. "Last night when I asked you what had occurred between you and Sophia, you told me it was nothing. That she'd gone into the house ahead of you and you didn't see her again."

Devon didn't know what to say. He hadn't wanted to lie to Adam last night, and he especially didn't want to lie to him now. But betraying Sophia's trust, admitting what had happened between them last night was even worse than keeping things from Adam. Besides, if he actually admitted that he'd been on his knees in front of her naked body, he wouldn't make it out of this room alive, and he wouldn't even blame Adam for it.

All of that, however, was secondary to the fact that Sophia was clearly upset and had run from him, and he wanted nothing more than to go to her and fix whatever the hell was wrong.

Panic clawed at him as he imagined her out there talking herself out of admitting that they had a connection, that they had something special. He'd promised her that he'd ask nothing of her save for a duchess and a motherly figure for the children but— well, things had changed. For him at least. Had that been what had overset her so? Had he somehow given himself away before he'd had the chance to say anything? Before he'd even had the chance to know his own feelings, his own mind?

He didn't know the answers to any of the questions flying through his mind. But what he did know was that standing here with Adam wasn't going to help Sophia.

"I need to go after her," he said in lieu of a real answer, but Adam's jaw was clenched, as were his fists, and Devon knew the former soldier wasn't about to just step aside. "Adam, I swear to you I did no harm to her, and I never would. But right now, she is out there clearly upset and alone, so please, step aside and let me find her."

Adam stared him down for what felt like eons before he suddenly muttered a black oath. "What the hell are you doing, Farnshire?" the marquis snapped. "Two weeks ago, you couldn't keep your damned hands to yourself, but I gave you the benefit of the doubt. You used our friendship to *force my hand* and give you the benefit of the doubt. And truth be told, I thought it would be good for you. For both of you. It even looked like you might be coming to care for each other."

"That's true." The marchioness suddenly piped up reminding Devon that she was still in the room. "You're the first human male she's ever deigned to spend time with."

Devon frowned, momentarily distracted by trying to figure out if he'd been insulted or not. But one look at Adam's glower reminded him just how serious this had the potential to be. He was well aware of how much Adam had turned a blind eye these past weeks, allowing him to spend an inordinate amount of time alone with Sophia, or even just with the children for company. Francesca wouldn't have cared either way, he knew, but Adam felt a sense of protectiveness for his sister-in-law, and Devon couldn't feel anything other than grateful for that.

"But this has gone on long enough, Devon. You either get an answer from her or that's it. You're done spending time alone with her. There'll be a maid or footman stationed in every room, and I'll sleep outside my bedchamber myself if I have to."

All at once, Devon was furious. He didn't know if it was because Adam was implying that Sophia needed protection from him, or because the idea of being anywhere near her bedchamber sent the familiar flame of lust licking at his skin even now at this most inopportune time. Hell, maybe it was just that he was terrified that Adam would stick to his word and he'd run out of time with her. Either way, his black fury was a welcome distraction from the fear.

"What the hell do you take me for?" he snapped, even though he had no real right to, not after what they'd done last night. "You think I'm lurking around every corner, lifting your sister-in-law's skirts every chance I get?"

"Well, this was an excellent time to come into the morning room. Just what has our Sophia been doing with her skirts?"

A female voice that didn't belong to Sophia or Francesca sounded from the doorway, and Devon's stomach dropped to his Hessians as he took in the crowd that had assembled there. The quip came from the beautiful blond, grinning from ear to ear, while the black-haired man with a hand on her shoulder shot daggers at him.

Behind them was an ethereal brunette who looked so much like Sophia his heart squeezed as he took in her wide-eyed stare.

Sophia's sisters, he remembered. The viscountess and the countess. And that meant that the men glaring at him were yet more protective brothers-in-law.

"That's an excellent question, Hope," the viscount who was bringing up the rear stepped forward then fixed Devon with an unblinking stare. "And I think you should answer it, Your Grace."

Chapter Twenty-One

"I HAVE TO hand it to you; you've picked a positively delicious specimen to scandalize Adam with."

"A duke no less. Mama won't rest until she's tried to marry you off now, Sophia."

Sophia spun around to see Elle and Hope grinning at her, Francesca in the middle of them, both looking oddly smug. With a squeal of delight, she ran over and threw her arms around first Elle and then Hope.

She'd quite forgotten that the rest of the family was arriving today. With only a week left until Christmas, there was still so much to do to prepare for the occasion, but all sense of time had quite simply slipped away from her.

"Where are the children?" she asked, studiously avoiding her sisters' shrewd looks. "I cannot believe they aren't already out here demanding to see my horses," she said with a laugh though it sounded brittle, even to her own ears.

"They would have been, but they found the duke's charges with some stolen gingerbread so they all ran off to the nursery before they were caught." Hope grinned, clearly proud of the children's mischief. Elodie looked a little less impressed but seemed happy to drop it as her chocolate-brown eyes bore into Sophia.

"So, tell us, why did Adam look like he was about to murder your scrumptious Scot?" Hope asked, moving to sit on the swing

Sophia had just vacated.

The swing was wide enough for all four sisters to sit side by side, the plank of wood tied to the giant oak by such thick rope that Sophia felt sure it would hold all their weight. She dropped down beside Hope, genuine fear filling her heart.

"Wait, what?" she gasped. "They were fighting?"

"Less fighting, more talk of the duke lifting your skirts in every room of the house," Hope said nonchalantly. "I must say, I'm impressed. Every room in Heywood Manor? Though, does that include servant quarters? Because if it's only the main rooms, it's rather less remarkable, though no less fun, I'm sure."

Francesca sat on Sophia's other side, pushing against her until she shuffled down and made room for Elodie. When they were all sitting in a row facing the rolling, snow-covered meadows of Halton, Sophia knew there would be no escaping an inquisition.

"He hasn't lifted my skirts in every room of the house, Hope," she bit out then leaned forward to turn an accusing eye on Elodie. "And why aren't you scolding her?" she demanded. "Don't you want to give a sermon on inappropriate language or something?"

Elle smiled that serene smile of hers and shrugged her shoulders. "Honestly, after all this time, I give up. She's Gideon's problem now." Hope stuck her tongue out. "And besides, I'm simply dying to hear about what's gone on here, Sophia. I truly didn't think anyone would get under your skin."

"Her skirts, Elle," Hope added unhelpfully. "Her skirts."

Sophia smacked Hope's shoulder but all that did was earn her a smack back.

"Cheska, this is your house. And you can usually sniff out scandal like a bloodhound, so tell us—has our little sister thrown herself down a path of ill-repute?" Elodie turned her attention to a thus far quiet Francesca.

"And did it least sound like she had fun doing it?" Hope asked with a comical leer.

Sophia tried in vain to maintain her annoyance but the truth was her sisters had always been incorrigible, and historically, she'd always joined in so she couldn't be truly angry with them. It just felt a little less fun when the boot was on the other leg, so to speak. How her sisters had all gone through this and lived to tell the tale she didn't know. But right now, she was more worried about Devon being alone with her three brothers-in-law than she was about her gossiping sisters.

"You don't think Adam is truly angry with him do you, Cheska?"

"Oh yes," she answered breezily. "He's furious. But he's hardly the one you need to worry about. Christian overheard him, too, and you know what he's like. I'm surprised we haven't heard pistols already."

Sophia groaned and dropped her head into her hands. "Elle, you need to do something about your husband. Christian still acts as though I'm a little girl and not a woman full grown."

"Don't worry, I won't allow him to murder the duke. But, Sophia," she reached across Cheska's rounded stomach to clasp Sophia's hand in her own, "you must tell us what is going on here."

Sophia's heart was hammering, those damned butterflies dancing an entire ballet in her stomach. But she knew that confiding in her sisters was probably for the best. They'd all been through their own tribulations with their husbands. Elle had stowed away in Christian's carriage and spent weeks alone with him traveling between inns. Hope—well, Hope had been Hope and had been practically naked in front of Gideon before she'd even known who he was. And Adam had been so altered by the war that it had taken all Francesca's efforts to just break through his torment to find the love inside of him.

But wasn't that the difference though? Christian had fallen in love with Elle on the road, and Sophia had never seen someone so besotted with his wife; Gideon would do anything for Hope. His devotion to her was evident every second one spent in his company. And Adam's love for Cheska was almost obscene in its intensity. Trials of the heart were surely a lot easier to overcome when the person you were having them with actually loved you.

"I've done something stupid," she finally admitted, unable to raise her voice above a whisper.

"Do we need to get you out of Halton?" Elle asked immediately, unquestioning loyalty in her eyes.

"Or get rid of someone?" Francesca asked, a little too enthusiastically.

"Or do we need to distract our husbands so you can have a fabulously immoral rendezvous with the dashing duke?" Hope asked with a waggle of her eyebrows.

Sophia laughed despite herself but without quite knowing why, her laugh soon became a sob.

"Oh, darling." Elodie squeezed the hand she was still clutching, Cheska wrapped an arm around her waist, and Hope leaned her head on her shoulder and suddenly she was transported back to when they were girls, surrounding each other in warmth and support, willing to stick by each other always. "What can you have done to upset you so?" Elle asked.

"I think—no, I *know* I love him and it's the worst thing that could have happened."

The sisters sat in silence for a moment or two not questioning the paradoxical sentence because, at one point or another, every one of them had felt the same way. They didn't try to pepper her with questions or tell her she was being foolish. No, they simply sat letting Sophia cry her tears before Hope, ever the romance-crazed hellion, piped up yet again. "When you said you were a *woman* now," she asked, "how womanly are we talking?"

"Not now, Hope," Elodie scolded.

There was another moment of silence before Francesca leaned her head back to whisper to Hope loud enough to wake the dead. "Do we need to get rid of the *duke*?"

Sophia just rolled her eyes and pretended she couldn't hear them. But even if she was ignoring them, it was nice to have them here all the same.

※》》《《

DEVON HAD THOUGHT that dealing with Adam would be difficult but dealing with Adam and the other two lords currently sitting in seething silence was slightly more of a challenge. There'd been nothing more than stilted silence interspersed with chitchat about the driving conditions since the Templeworth ladies had run off to find their sister.

At least he knew she wasn't alone, Devon thought, though he would much rather be with her than sitting here under the watchful eye of the three other peers.

"I can't say I'm all that thrilled," the viscount broke the silence, and Devon prepared himself for a barrage of questions that he wasn't sure he was ready to answer. But then, to his surprise, Brentford focused his glare on Adam. "Sophia was under your care, which means whatever the hell was going on here was under *your* nose."

Adam scowled at Devon, the look accusatory before he sighed and turned his attention to the viscount. "What can I say?" he drawled, though his demeanor was anything but relaxed. "Controlling anything Sophia does is akin to controlling a battalion. I should know."

"I'd imagine a battalion might be easier," Claremont snorted, and to Devon's relief, the others chuckled in agreement.

That relief was short lived, however, when all three sets of eyes turned back to him once more. "Devon," Adam's tone brooked no argument and though Devon wasn't intimidated by anyone, including the three formidable lords sizing him up now, he knew that he should explain himself. For one thing he could respect that the gentlemen had Sophia's best interests at heart, and he would never begrudge people who cared about what happened to her. But for another, far more important thing, if he got his way and Sophia consented to marry him, these gentlemen would be his family and as such he owed them his respect. "You knew you were playing a dangerous game. And now the game has to come to an end."

Devon kept a calm, easy mask on his face but inside he was raging against what he knew was coming. He'd never wanted Sophia like this. Her control taken away. Forced to be his because he couldn't keep his damned hands off her. She deserved better than that. Sure, when he hadn't known much about her, he'd thought there wasn't a woman in Christendom who wouldn't have jumped at the chance to be a duchess.

But as time had gone on, as he'd watched her with the children, as he'd gotten to know her smile and her hot temper, her stubbornness and love of horses, her passion, her taste, her scent—he'd no longer wanted her as a means to an end. He wanted her for himself. For Devon the man, not Farnshire the duke.

"I have no idea what the hell *game* you're talking about, but it's irrelevant. We heard enough to know that something has gone on between you and Sophia and honestly, having gone through this with Hope and Francesca already, I don't think my heart could take hearing the details. So, you'll marry her, and we can lie and tell ourselves that nothing untoward happened between you before the wedding."

And there it was. A guaranteed way to ensure Sophia would hate him for the rest of their lives.

"You're forgetting something, Christian," Claremont, who'd stayed relatively quiet up until this point now spoke up, though the glare he shot Devon was proof that he wasn't taking his side in anything.

"What's that?"

"Sophia," Claremont said, a smirk playing around his mouth. "Do I need to remind you what that little hellion is capable of? Remember you tried to force her to join you and that sniveling little worm Sir Alonso at the theater, and she glued the doors of all your carriages shut?"

Despite the seriousness of the situation, Devon had to clench his jaw to keep from laughing. Of course she'd done something so—well, so Sophia.

Brentford swore and rolled his eyes.

"Or when she joined us in Cornwall and I didn't want Hope to go sea-bathing during her lying-in period and she set fire to my drawing room to create a diversion?" At that, Devon couldn't contain his own oath, and Claremont's eyes snapped to him. There was a grudging respect in their dark depths and even a trace of humor, though Devon imagined he didn't find it all that funny at the time. "She had it all under control," he drawled. "That's what the little demon told me when I finally tracked her and Hope down on the beach."

As one, they all turned their eyes to Adam who looked reluctant to say anything but eventually, he sighed and shrugged. "I tried to stop her attending a makeshift gambling den when we were back at Heywood," he said grimly. "She used the bedding of every damned bedchamber in the Abbey and climbed out the window. I found her in the rosebushes hours later drunk as a sailor and casting up her accounts. *And*," he added with a laugh as though he still couldn't quite believe it, "she'd lost a small fortune that I ended up having to pay for her since she couldn't bloody remember it."

Good lord, she was wild. Devon had known, of course. Had experienced some of her stubbornness firsthand. But this? It was bordering on insane. So why did he find it so damned attractive?

"We've all suffered at the hands of our darling little sister-in-law," Claremont said, turning his attention back to Brentford. "So how in the hell do you propose we make her do anything she doesn't want to do?"

Brentford stared at Devon for an age. Until Devon himself broke the silence. "I should warn you," he said softly but firmly, "I have no intention of trying to force Sophia to do *anything* she doesn't want to do."

Adam snorted beside him. "As though you could." Which was fair. Especially after hearing of her escapades.

"Then I suppose the question is—is there any chance that she'll want you?"

Chapter Twenty-Two

"**I**F ONE OF you breathes a word to Mama, I will dance on your graves." All three of her sisters froze and blinked in shock before their faces broke into grins. Except Elodie's. Elodie had paled ever so slightly.

"You're being terribly dramatic, Sophia. 'Tis just a nice, quiet family dinner."

Outside the door of her bedchamber came the noise of the children screeching and laughing as they tore up and down the corridor.

"Very well," she sighed, rolling her eyes. "A family dinner. Nothing quiet about it."

Sophia chuckled softly as she ran a discerning eye over herself in the looking glass. Heather's giggle sounded like a bell in the midst of the chaos, and then Finn's laughter, clear and loud and sounding exactly as a child's should followed it, and she felt as though her heart might crack in half. They'd come to mean so much to her. She loved them, she realized. Not just because they were wonderful and had been through so much in their short lives but because they were a part of Devon.

And if possible, she loved him even more because of how he'd opened his heart to them. When they'd first arrived in Halton, she'd seen the gap between Devon and Finn, especially. It had been clear that he loved them and wanted what was best for them, that had been the reason for his unorthodox proposal after all. But now? Now he skated with them and picked Christmas garlands with them, taught them to ride, and chased them around on all fours pretending to be a monstrous creature. Just the other day she'd caught him keeping watch while they'd snuck applies pies from the kitchen. Now that they'd discovered the gingerbread, there'd be no stopping them.

"Look at you going all moon-eyed. I take it you're thinking of that giant specimen of dukedom downstairs?"

"Actually, I was just thinking that it was nice to hear the children laugh and play." Hope merely raised a brow and waited until Sophia gave in.

"Fine. Then my mind might have wandered to Devon."

Hope's laugh merged with Cheska's and Elle's. "Trust me," she said running a hand down her own gown, "I understand the affliction. Even after all these years I get giddy just thinking about Gideon, let alone being in the same room as him."

"I'm the same with Christian," Elodie admitted, her cheeks growing a becoming shade of pink. "Sometimes when he looks at me, I genuinely worry I'll turn into a puddle at his feet."

"Oh, lord. Sometimes I have to tell Adam not to smile at me the way he does or I won't be responsible for my actions. Especially now," she tacked on wryly, rubbing a hand over her rounded stomach.

Sophia had never minded her sisters' frankness about their bedroom activities but now that she'd experienced it, or at least some of it, firsthand, she could agree with everything they were saying. And there was no point in denying it, either, for they could surely see it in the way her eyes glazed over as she remembered Devon's lips against her flesh, his tongue and fingers bringing about such wicked pleasure.

The sound of nannies and maids rounding up the children sounded outside the bedchamber and dragged Sophia's mind from the gutter. Studiously ignoring her sisters' knowing glances, she ran a final eye over her navy-blue satin gown. She hadn't left herself much time this evening to get ready for dinner. The children had finally tracked her down as she'd made the journey back to the manor house with her sisters. Inevitably the rest of the day had been spent in the stables with her allowing them all to ride, and feed the horses, and even help to muck out the stables. Then they'd demanded that she play in the snow with them for so long that they all nearly froze solid, and she had to hurry them back to the house as the snow fell thick and heavy all around them. It hadn't stopped snowing since, and judging from the howling wind and the thick white frost on the windows, it was shaping up to be quite a blizzard out there.

She tried not to feel worried or hurt that Devon hadn't come to find her, but she couldn't deny that she'd missed having him around today. Besides, she was about to see him at dinner and while it wouldn't exactly be fun with her brothers-in-law no doubt glaring at him from one end of the table and her mother fawning at him from the other, she still wanted to see him if only to know that he'd survived an afternoon with her family.

And as she hurried down the stairs, she thought of what her sisters had said. How freely they spoke of their love for their husbands, how much quiet joy was etched on each of their faces. Even Francesca who had been the most rigidly independent woman in England had allowed herself to love Adam and be loved fiercely in return. Now when they entered the drawing room her sisters would be showered in love and affection and because of her own stubbornness, she wouldn't be.

Would it really be so bad, she wondered, to say yes and marry him even knowing that he didn't love her as she loved him? They hadn't discussed loyalty or fidelity but, surely, he wouldn't use her so ill as to parade mistresses around in front of her? And there was no denying their heat. Wouldn't that be enough for him? She almost had herself convinced that she could waltz into that room right now and tell him yes but then a niggling voice awoke in the back of her mind. *And if he falls in love? What then? Loyalty won't stop him giving his heart to another.*

The idea made her heart ache. He'd told her that he didn't

believe in love. That he didn't really have the time or inclination to have it in his life. But Hope had said the same thing when Gideon's past had caught up to him. Christian hadn't wanted to marry Elodie at first. Adam hadn't thought himself incapable of love until he'd fallen for Francesca. And then there was her. Sophia. Who'd tumbled headfirst into a love so all-consuming that it was taking over her entire life.

Maybe she could consider marrying him knowing that the love she felt might never be reciprocated. But she didn't think she could live with the risk of him loving someone else.

DEVON FELT THE weight of inevitable doom weigh him down as he stood in Adam's drawing room and awaited Sophia's arrival. If the other lords insisted on forcing his hand, he might lose her. He knew this and damn it, Adam knew it, too. They all should.

He didn't blame them for being protective but Christ, why couldn't they trust that he knew best? It had been a mistake, he thought now, refusing to admit his true feelings for her to her brothers-in-law. Telling himself that she deserved to hear it from him before anyone else.

The drawing room door opened and there she was, swept up in the crowd of her sisters, who broke off one by one into the waiting arms of their husbands. Devon cast a quick glance over them all. It was uncommon in the *ton* for there to be love matches. Not unheard of but for peers as powerful as those in this room, certainly relatively unusual. Yet every man in here was in love with their wives and judging from the smiles and heated glances the feeling was very much mutual.

A lance of white-hot jealousy ripped through him. He wanted that. He did. He'd never wanted it before but now that Sophia was in his life? Damn it all, he wanted it. *Craved* it. But only because of her. Only with her. And he was terrified that it was going to be ripped away from him before he got the chance to explain.

If nothing else, she deserved to hear the truth of his feelings. That she had gone from someone he thought the children might like to the woman he knew he would love every single second of every single day. And she needed to know before things went wrong for them.

"Sophia." He prowled across the room toward her, knowing that he must look as desperate as he suddenly felt from the way her eyes widened.

"Devon, are you well?" she asked, her eyes impossibly blue against the color of her dress boring into him. But then she smiled a little, her expression relaxing. "Oh, I understand. My brothers-in-law have given you a hard time, haven't they?"

"Something like that," he said weakly, trying and failing to smile. "But that's not important right now. I need to talk to you." It took everything in him not to reach out and touch her, but he kept his fists clenched by his sides, knowing that the slightest thing could set off one of the pack of guard dogs no doubt watching his every move.

"Well? Speak then," she laughed.

"No. I—alone," he rasped. "Let's go somewhere so that we can talk. So I can explain."

She frowned in confusion, and he didn't blame her. He was acting a little strangely. He needed to calm down. But he was so scared of losing her. Of somehow undoing all the trust he'd gained over the past couple of weeks.

"Explain what?" she asked, demanded really. "You haven't even told me I look beautiful," she added with a raised brow and a faux scowl on her face. And God, but he loved her so much in that moment.

"You are the most beautiful thing in the world, Sophia Templeworth, as you well know. In a satin gown or breeches and everything in between." And then, because he was a foolish bastard and couldn't help himself, he dropped his tone and leaned forward to growl in her ear. "But especially when you're completely naked and writhing against my tongue."

He felt her breathing hitch as she reached out and clasped the sleeve of his dinner jacket, gripping it tightly as though she didn't trust her legs any longer, and the lust that coursed through his veins at the reaction nearly blinded him.

She turned her head slightly so that the lips that had been by her ear scraped along her jaw landing agonizingly, tantalizingly close to those plump, red lips. He knew he should pull back, that this was akin to sealing their fates. And she didn't deserve that. She didn't deserve to have her choices taken from her.

He was so close that he saw a myriad of emotions flicker through her eyes. There was lust, a brief moment of indecision, even perhaps fear. But then they filled with so much tenderness that it stole his breath clean away and hope to burst inside his chest. He reached out to clasp her hand, determined to pull her out of the room so he could finally confess what was in his heart and ask her to be his, for the right reasons this time.

But from across the room, he heard Brentford's voice. "I hope you told her that she's marrying you, Farnshire. Otherwise, you'd better get your damned hands off her."

There was an endless moment of shocked silence before it was broken by yet another voice. And Devon winced as Mrs. Templeworth's screech shattered the quiet permeating the room.

"The duke! Sophia, you are marrying the duke? Finally, you've done something right."

Chapter Twenty-Three

SOPHIA DIDN'T KNOW how to respond to the maelstrom of emotions that were battering her. She'd gone from a moment of pure elation at what she thought she saw lurking in the depths of Devon's eyes, to confusion at Christian's oddly aggressive tone, to sheer horror as Mama's screams shattered her peace of mind.

I hope you told her that she's marrying you, Farnshire. That's what Christian had said. And she waited for Devon to say something. Even while Mama pulled out of her neck playing at being the doting mother, she watched Devon's face. Waited for him to explain what was going on.

But he just stared at her. So, she turned her attention to Christian. Beside him Gideon and Adam were looking on rather sheepishly, and she knew then that they must have spent the afternoon discussing *her* life and deciding what *her* future was going to be. Her sisters at least looked confused but willing to do battle.

"What do you mean *told* me I was marrying him, Christian?" she asked, her voice deathly quiet and portraying a calmness that she absolutely didn't feel.

Christian opened his mouth, shut it again then sighed and stepped forward, his hands splayed as though she were holding a pistol to him or something. "Sophia, you know that we cannot just stand by and allow you to, to—"

"To what?" Cheska demanded, a brow raised at Christian.

By this point, Elodie, Hope, and Cheska had removed themselves from their husbands' arms and now they moved as one to surrounded her, Hope none-too-gently pushing Devon out of the way, and Elodie subtly bypassing their mother so she could keep Sophia away from her.

"Sweetheart, you know I was willing to allow this to play out. At your request I might add," Adam said now appealing to Francesca. "But you must see it's gone on long enough."

"That's not for you to decide," Hope spat out, her eyes furious as they stared at Gideon. To his credit he stood his ground, only pulling at his cravat.

"We won't stand for anyone taking advantage of Sophia," he said, his tone defensive.

"Because you all behaved like paragons in the past?" Sophia was momentarily distracted and impressed by Elodie, usually the peacemaker, speaking up.

Christian snapped a glance to Mama, but she was clearly not listening to anything, mumbling to herself as she practically salivated on the Aubusson rug. She would have the whole of Halton covered with the news tomorrow. News that Sophia hadn't bloody agreed to.

"We're just trying to look out for you, Sophia. Because we care about you and what happens to you, and we don't want anyone taking advantage of you."

She could only stare at them all. She wanted to rail against them but stopped herself because deep down, as misguided and interfering and overbearing as they were, she knew Christian was speaking honestly. This *was* because they cared about her and didn't want her to be taken advantage of.

But they should know her well enough by now not to try to tell her what to do. It was maddening that they didn't.

Worse than any of that, though, was the fact that Devon had clearly discussed this with them and had gone along with this. After his blunder when he'd first announced that they were to be wed, she'd stupidly started to trust him. To trust that he had grown to know her. Really know her. All the parts that she had never shared with anyone else. The parts that she thought he'd come to care about. He had made her believe that her stubbornness was somehow endearing to him. Had made her think that he respected her and *liked* her at least well enough to understand her desire to be mistress of her own fate.

Day after day they'd talked, they'd bonded. Or so she had thought.

Was it all for naught? Had it all gone away as soon as he'd seen the chance to manipulate the situation? Had he delighted in the fact that her brothers-in-law would put pressure on her to marry him? So many questions swirled inside her.

And still Devon didn't speak.

"I'm not going to be *told* to marry anyone, Christian," she finally broke her own silence. And though she addressed her eldest brother-in-law, she kept her eyes on Devon. "And you should know better than that."

Devon swallowed thickly. "Sophia, I explained that I wanted to speak to you privately."

"Yes, and then you manhandled her in front of us." Gideon's reply was smooth, but Devon still gritted his teeth as he swung toward him.

"And I also told you that I wasn't going to stand by while you forced her hand."

"Yes, and then you manhandled her in front of us," Adam repeated Gideon's words. "Honestly, Devon, what the hell do you expect?"

Devon opened his mouth to answer back but Sophia had heard enough. She couldn't stand here listening to them argue, trying to figure out what exactly they'd agreed to or who had said what. She felt sick and upset. And listening to her mother's girlish giggles was doing nothing to calm her temper.

Suddenly she needed get away from them all. From Christian's bloody highhandedness, and Devon's look of concern, and even her sisters' voices as they joined the fray to yell at their respective husbands. It was a loud, noisy mess, and she needed quiet. She needed to *think*.

Without a word to any of them, she turned on her heel and ran from the drawing room planning on locking herself inside her bedchamber until her heart stopped its sickening hammering. But a screech of "Aunt Sophia" caught her attention and she looked up to see that the small army of Templeworth children had escaped their nannies and were bearing down upon her. But she couldn't face them just now. She just needed space. She needed to be alone.

The children started down the staircase, nannies and maids in their wake. And behind her, the door to the drawing room was flung open, Devon calling out to her, her sisters trying to push him out of the way.

It was too much. Too loud. Too *everything*.

She turned and ran. Shouts rang out behind her, but she ignored them all, darting to the back of the house. Nearly knocking poor Severin, who was likely on his way to announce dinner, off his feet, she bolted for the conservatory, gasping at the cold air before she'd even reached the door that led to the gardens. But still she ran.

Bursting onto the patio, she made a dash for the stables. Barely able to see through the snow, her satin slippers sank into the sodden ground and in seconds, her dress was soaked through with icy water. And still, she didn't slow. Her teeth chattered, the howling wind tore at her hair, the snow landed like ice on her bare arms yet on she ran.

By the time she reached the stables, she could no longer feel her feet and the only voice she could still hear over the wind was Devon's, hoarse and panicked. She hadn't planned on riding in this weather, of course, she hadn't; it was madness. Yet hearing that he was closing in on her made her irrational. And even as some small, still functioning part of her brain yelled at her to stop being so foolish, she grabbed a saddle and practically threw it onto Ares.

It was the work of a moment to saddle and bridle Ares, but her fingers were so numb through her white satin gloves that she couldn't even be sure she'd done it properly. Devon's giant frame suddenly filled the doorway of the stable, blocking out the feeble light from the lanterns hanging there.

"Sophia. What are you doing?" he gasped as he rushed toward her. She jumped onto Ares's back, scrambling to right herself and sit astride in the silly gown. Without a word, she kicked the horse's flanks and shot out of the stables past where Devon was desperately reaching for her.

Her only thought was escape. That and hoping that she didn't make Ares too cold. The snowstorm made it impossible to see more than inches in front of her, but she knew the grounds. There was a line of bushes ahead, bushes that she'd cleared a thousand times. She could do it with her eyes closed, so she could do it now.

Squinting through the snow, she caught sight of the vague outline just seconds before they reached them, and she pulled with all her might, praying that Ares would clear it.

The sound of Devon screaming her name filled the night air, sounding as though it had been ripped from his soul itself. And for a split second she was confused by the terror in it. She'd never heard such a tortured sound.

But then she felt it. The lurch of a saddle that shouldn't have moved. It seemed as though time slowed as Ares landed and she went careening over the head of the beast and careening toward the snow packed ground.

The last thing she heard was a sickening crunch. The last thing she felt was a blinding pain. And then, a soothing black dulling the edge of her senses. Somewhere in the distant she heard her name. Over and over again it was screamed like a litany. But a darkness was sweeping toward her, blissful nothingness just waiting to take her away. So, she succumbed, and the world went quiet.

>>><<<

DEVON HAD NEVER known fear until that moment. Never known grief the likes of which was threatening to smother him as he fought his way through that damned bush and caught sight of Sophia's still, broken body laid out in the snow.

Even in the dark he could see the pool of crimson, a shocking, sickening contrast to the brilliant whiteness that lay all around her. Dropping to his knees, he reached out a shaking hand to cup her face. Her skin was ice cold, her lips an alarming shade of blue.

Panic swirled and eddied inside him making it impossible to think clearly. He didn't know if moving her would do more damage, but he couldn't leave her in the damned snow. This was all his fault. If he'd just been honest, if he'd just opened his heart and told her how he felt when he knew instead of being scared that she wouldn't reciprocate his feelings, she'd be inside now with her sisters.

A broken, ragged sob sounded, and it took him a moment to realize it was coming from him. "Please," he whispered to the broken doll she'd become. "Please be well." He was too scared to feel for a pulse, knowing that if there was none then he would die right here alongside her. Despite the fact that he was needed by Heather and Finn, by the people who relied on the duchy for their livelihoods, he knew he wouldn't survive Sophia being taken from this world.

"Sophia lass, please, *please*," he begged. "I will never see you again if that is what you need. Just don't leave this world. I can't live in it if you're not in it."

There was nothing, no movement, no sound. Just him and the storm and his universe crumbling down around him. Ares was long gone, but he couldn't waste time trying to find the mount.

Shedding his jacket, he didn't even feel the snow and wind through the thin material of his waistcoat. He couldn't feel anything. It felt as though his mind simply emptied of thought, his heart of feeling. In some dark recess of his mind, he knew that he had probably entered some sort of state of shock, but he welcomed the embrace of numbness. He couldn't help her if he couldn't function.

Lifting her too-still body into his arms, another sob was wrenched from his chest at the hair matted and bloodied on her temple. He looked down and saw the root of one of the bushes right where her head had been.

He would never forgive himself for this. Never.

Making sure her head was pressed against his chest, he turned and hurried through the snow back to the manor house, praying to God to save her, even if she hated him for the rest of his life, every step of the way.

Chapter Twenty-Four

"SOPHIA!"

"Oh, my goodness."

"Damn it all."

"Quick, someone fetch the doctor."

A cacophony of sound broke out around Devon as he burst through the doors of the manor house. He couldn't make out who was saying what, but he didn't particularly care. A set of hands reached out as though to take Sophia from his arms, but he ground out a black warning and they disappeared.

Barking at people to get out of his way, he headed for the staircase and Sophia's bedchamber. It was a testament to the seriousness of the situation that nobody objected, and the panic that he'd held at bay broke like a dam had burst. Setting her on the bed, he nearly cast up his accounts as he took in the blood-stain already leaking across the satin pillowcases.

He felt as though he were watching the events play out from somewhere above them all. There was her bloody mother screaming for her smelling salts in the corner as though she were somehow the priority. Her sisters were alternating between crying and shouting orders. And there he was, covered in her blood, his linen shirt soaked through with it, kneeling at her side and weeping.

"Devon, Dr. Pearse is on his way. He'll do everything he can, I swear it." Adam's voice sounded fierce and harsh in his ear, his hand clamped on Devon's shoulder.

Dr. Pearse. The man who'd been trying to court her a life-time ago. Now probably the only thing standing between her and death. If he saved her then, perhaps, he would deserve her. He'd deserve the bloody world. Devon would hand over every title, every house, every coin to the weak-chinned doctor if it meant Sophia opening those blue eyes.

He didn't know how long he knelt there with her stiff, cold hand clasped in both of his. But then came a set of hands, dragging him away. Someone tried to coax him away to change out of his wet, bloody clothes but he threatened bodily harm to anyone who touched him, so he was left alone, save for a glass filled to the brim with brandy pressed into his hands. He downed it in one swallow and almost immediately, it was refilled.

Dr. Pearse arrived and tried to get him to leave the room, but one growl was enough to shut the man up. Devon stood silently watching, silently praying as the doctor examined every inch of her. Ordering her to be stripped from her wet clothes, Devon finally conceded to moving out of the way when the doctor explained that she could just as easily die from exposure to the cold as she could from any injury she'd sustained.

He stood outside the bedchamber with the rest of her family save for her mother, who'd insisted on being taken to a guest chamber to rest after the shock. Devon could have happily wrung her neck, but he didn't care enough about her to bother.

He answered her family's questions as best he could, his voice raspy and coarse from the way he'd been screaming her name but even as he spoke, his mind was in that room.

After eons, the door finally opened, and the doctor signaled for them to enter. The candlelight flickered over Sophia's face and hair, the only part of her now visible among layers of blankets. His heart clenched painfully at the white bandage that now covered the left side of her temple, another on her right wrist. The fire was roaring, making the room almost stifling hot, and he listened with half an ear as Dr. Pearse explained in subdued tones that she must be kept as warm as possible.

"Why isn't she awake?" he asked never once removing his eyes from her.

It took so long for the doctor to answer that Devon dragged his gaze from Sophia and pinned the smaller man with it instead.

"Head wounds are notoriously difficult," he began, his voice so somber that it put the fear of God into Devon. "She lost a lot of blood, and the truth is, we have no way of knowing what damage might have been done. She has bruising around her ribs and her wrist is quite badly sprained. She—" He paused, taking a breath as if steeling himself to deliver a blow, and Devon's entire body iced over as he waited for it to come. "She had a nasty injury and coupled with the cold, well, the truth is that I'm not sure how long it will take her to awaken. Or—"

"No." The word was out before he even realized he had spoken. But Devon had a feeling he knew what was coming next, and he couldn't stand it. He couldn't. He tore at the strands of his hair as he stared down at the woman who owned every part of him, who had become his reason to breathe, his reason to live.

"Just tell us." Francesca's voice trembled, and for one mad moment Devon wanted to roar at her to just shut up so they wouldn't have to hear this. So they could pretend that all was well and that Sophia would be on her feet and in the stables first thing in the morning.

"Or even if she will," Pearse finally said, his voice apologetic.

The pain that ravaged Devon took the strength clean from his body, and he dropped to his knees right there where he stood. Activity once more broke out around him with questions being thrown at the doctor, hasty instructions being given to pale-faced maids, and quiet sobs interspersing it all.

Through it all, he watched her. Through it all, he bargained with God for her soul. Through it all, he felt every single tiny part of his heart crumble to dust.

⋙⋘

THE LIGHT WAS blinding and so much worse than the comforting darkness that Sophia wished it would just go away. Her head was pounding, and her entire body felt so stiff that she was afraid if she moved her limbs would snap.

And Lord, but she was thirsty. Her mouth felt as though it were filled with sand.

She didn't know where she was, and she knew that she should open her eyes to check but her lids were so heavy, and the light was so very bright.

"Devon, come and eat something. I'll sit with her in case she wakes."

Elodie's voice drifted toward Sophia as though it were on a cloud. She'd said Devon. Devon was here? Sitting with her? All at once, she was desperate to open her eyes despite how much it might hurt. She wanted to see him. But it felt as though she were underwater swimming for a surface that just wouldn't appear. And she was so very tired from trying.

"I'll wait a little longer." His voice—she'd never heard it sound so hollow, so defeated. The Scottish brogue was more pronounced than ever, and she was desperate to reach out, to comfort him. She didn't know why he sounded so dreadfully sad, but it hurt to hear it.

"You've been here for two days," Elodie said, sounding as though she'd come closer. "You've barely eaten, you haven't slept. Dr. Pearse," Elodie stopped talking suddenly and inhaled a gulp of air. And when she spoke again her voice sounded filled with tears. Sophia's confusion only grew. "Dr. Pearse said it could take weeks. You can't sit here for weeks."

They grew quiet, and Sophia could hear nothing save for a strange rasping sound. And then she realized that it was Devon. It sounded as though he were crying but surely that wasn't possible. Her heart hurt for him but that surface she was trying to reach was drifting further and further away.

"I can," he said but his voice was muffled, and she could barely hear. "I will sit here for weeks if I must. For *years*. I need to be here when she wakes. I need to see her open her eyes."

There was a soft sigh, a click as though a door were being shut and then nothing. Sophia began to sink into the darkness again but right before she went, she was sure she felt the brush of lips against her brow.

"Come back to me, lass. Please come back to me. I love you. I need you with me. Please." The words were gut-wrenching, and she wanted to tell him that she was trying but the exhaustion was all-consuming.

She would rest now, she told herself. And she would tell him tomorrow.

Chapter Twenty-Five

THREE DAYS, SIX hours, and forty-two minutes. That's how long it had been since Sophia had fallen from the horse. And aside from seeing to his ablutions, Devon hadn't left her side for it.

He'd long since learned to ignore the aches and cramps he had from folding six feet and five inches into a tiny chair. He'd long since stopped trying to distract himself with books or the papers or even getting blind drunk.

The only reason he wasn't in the same bloody clothes was because Christian, Gideon, and Adam had made him bathe and change telling him that he'd be no good to Sophia if he didn't. And while their wives had been fussing over him and ensuring that he ate, they had been keeping him fed on brandy which he appreciated. But he'd stopped short of being foxed, wanting a clear head when she awoke. And she would wake up. Despite what he knew the others whispered about sometimes, despite what her horrible mother had wailed when she'd finally deigned to come in and see her youngest daughter, he knew Sophia Templeworth was far too stubborn to let go of life before she'd truly had the chance to live it.

And being the horse-mad woman that she was, she certainly wasn't going to shuffle off the mortal coil because of a riding accident. He just knew she wouldn't.

It was Christmas in a few days. Adam and Francesca had been

planning to throw something of a winter festival this year with lots of activities for the family and the locals. It should have started today, culminating in a ball on Christmas Eve. A ball that he'd hoped they might announce a betrothal at. Of course, it was all cancelled now.

Outside the door, the distinctive sound of an army of little feet broke the stifling silence. The children, Sophia's nieces and nephews and Heather and Finn had all been so worried about her. And Devon had tried to comfort them, he really had. But any time he saw their little faces, he felt like howling in rage and fear and so he'd shut himself in here, relying on Sophia's family to keep them all distracted. And they were doing a wonderful job of it.

Every so often he'd stand at the window looking out at the grounds and inevitably there'd be some activity or other involving the children. Snowball fights and the building of entire snow villages, and sometimes just running around in circles trying to catch falling flakes on their tongues. They'd even gone skating with the viscount and viscountess yesterday. Their laughter and shouts of excitement had managed to bring a smile to his face, even as his heart clenched remembering his day of skating with Sophia.

She had brought so much joy to all their lives. Had shown him how to be what the children needed and, in turn, they'd blossomed under her love and care. How would he ever face them again if she didn't awaken? How would he ever learn to live with the guilt? How would he ever again experience joy if a light so bright was extinguished and gone from the world? He wouldn't. He couldn't.

Swallowing yet another lump in his throat, he moved to throw more logs on the fire, if only to break the monotony of sitting there and going slowly out of his mind.

Dr. Pearse visited twice a day, always declaring that she was no better and no worse. The only shred of good news had been that, somehow, she hadn't contracted a fever from being in the cold. Devon had clung to the positivity of that information for as long as possible but it hadn't been anywhere enough to stem the tide of worry and grief.

This morning when Dr. Pearse had conducted his interview, he'd asked to speak to the family downstairs. Devon had been torn between going with them and staying by Sophia's side. In the end he'd decided that he'd be likely to smash something if it was yet more bad news so he'd stayed here.

Not half an hour later, he'd heard the sisters squabbling outside the door about who should come in and face him. In the end, they'd decided that since Elodie was the nicest, she was the least likely to be roared at, so it was she who tiptoed into the room. Her eyes had gone straight to Sophia, a sadness that was becoming all too familiar dulling them.

She'd explained how Dr. Pearse had wanted to warn them of potential outcomes. Warn them that even if she awoke, the longer she stayed unconscious the higher the likelihood that she wouldn't come out of this unscathed. She might be altered forever, he'd said, in her mind. And they would just have to wait and see how that would manifest.

Devon hadn't left her side since. If she was changed, he vowed, he wouldn't love her any less. But what if she didn't recognize him? What if she didn't recognize *anything*? It was another worry to add to the ever-growing list.

He turned his eyes to the ormolu clock on the mantle. Three days, six hours, and forty-seven minutes. He despaired of it ever ending but had to believe that it would and that she would wake.

Taking his seat once more he reached out and clasped her hand before raising his eyes to her face.

And saw her own staring back at him.

EVERYTHING *HURT*. HER eyes, her head, her throat, her arm. But nothing hurt as much as seeing Devon crumple before her eyes. When she'd managed to pry them open, she'd found herself looking at the back of his head as he'd gazed out the window. And as she'd lain there trying to figure out what was going on, it had all suddenly come rushing back.

The argument with Christian. Her mad, foolish dash through a storm. And then Devon screaming her name, and Ares jumping, and the ground flying up to meet her. Well, it was no wonder she had a bloody headache.

Wincing at the stiffness in her arm, she reached up to press it gingerly against her head, not all that surprised to find a bandage there. She was probably black and blue. But right then she didn't particularly care.

She wanted answers. And water. And more answers. She thought she remembered whispered conversations, snippets of words, sniffles and sobs. Some of them from Devon. *Come back to me, lass. I love you.* Had she imagined those words? Dreamt them? The only way to find out was to ask but her voice didn't seem to want to cooperate and so she lay here, frustrated beyond belief, until he finally sat down, taken her hand, and faced her.

He'd grown so pale that he might have fallen to the floor if he hadn't already been sitting. His eyes filled with shock, then relief before he dropped his head to their clasped hands whispering over and over again. She caught the words "thank God" but not much else.

Working her throat, she finally managed to get a croak out. It wasn't even a word, but it was enough to have Devon's head snap up.

"What is it, lass? Are you in pain? Can you move? Can you remember who I am? Do you need a doctor? What am I saying, of course you need the bloody doctor. I'll just go—" Sophia could only stare at him as he rambled. She'd never seen him so flustered. So lacking in control. But as he jumped to his feet, she managed to stay him by squeezing his hand with all the unimpressive strength she could muster.

It hurt to move her head, but she managed a nod toward the pitcher beside the bed, and he mercifully caught on. "Water," he said. "Of course, you need water. I'm sorry." She watched as he lifted the jug with shaking hands and poured some into a glass, spilling most of it from the tremors. But some of it at least managed to land in the glass, and he sat on the edge of the bed, carefully sliding a hand under her head to lift it from the pillow.

"Here you go, sweetheart," he whispered holding the glass to her lips. She sipped at it then drank in greedy gulps until it was empty. He set it down on the table then turned back to her, gently pushing a lock of hair from her brow, his hand still shaking. Instead of pulling his hand away, he moved to cup her face, running a thumb along her cheekbone.

"Sophia, lass." He swallowed and a pit of dread formed in her stomach as she took in the sorrow on his face. Whatever he was going to say, it was clearly going to be awful, and she suddenly panicked that she'd somehow caused injury to Ares. If something had happened to Ares because she had thrown a tantrum she would never, ever forgive herself.

Steeling herself for what he was about to say, she stared into his face only just noticing how terrible he looked. He looked exhausted. He wore no cravat, no jacket, and his lawn shirt was rumpled and opened at his thick, strong neck. His hair was tousled as though he'd been running his hands through it, and his jaw was unshaven. But it was his eyes that caused her to catch her breath. They were so sad, so hollow. Reaching out, she grasped at the hand that wasn't holding her face as though it were the most precious china.

"Is it Ares?" she managed to get out, shocked at how rough her voice sounded.

The eyes that had been scanning every inch of her face snapped back to her own, and there was a flicker of some strong emotion in them. Maybe relief? "Is what Ares?" he asked carefully.

"D-did I hurt him?" To her horror, she felt her eyes filled with tears that immediately spilled out over her face.

Devon blinked down at her for a moment before his eyes filled with understanding. "No, no, lass. I swear it, the damned horse is fine and dandy. Unlike you."

"Do you promise?" she sniffed and he laughed softly, his eyes running over her face as though he were drinking her in.

"I promise. I swear it. He returned to the stables after, well after—"

"After my fall?" she whispered.

"You remember, then?" he asked. "You remember everything? The horse and the fall. And, and me? Your sisters?"

She frowned up at him, confusion filling her mind. "What? Don't be ridiculous, Devon. Of course, I remember you. Why wouldn't I?"

Her confusion only grew ten-fold when he laughed, the chuckle coming from deep inside him before suddenly he was leaning down only inches separating them, his eyes glowing in the afternoon light. "It's good to have you back, hellion," he whispered before pressing a soft kiss to her brow.

She tried not to feel disappointed that the kiss hadn't been longer or further south. But she was growing tired again and wasn't sure she'd have the energy for it. He opened his mouth to say something else, but at that moment, the door burst open and her sisters fell over each other into the room.

"Devon, we heard you laughing."

"Oh, my goodness, she's awake."

"Look at that scowl! She definitely remembers who she is."

The noise was deafening as her sisters descended on her, crying and laughing and talking all at once. Devon was given little choice but to move away from the bed but when she glanced up at him, he was smiling with such quiet joy that her heart filled to bursting.

He slipped from the room for a moment before coming back with Christian, Gideon, and Adam in tow.

"The doctor has been sent for," he called over the chaos

which only increased when all the children thundered into the room with squeals and shouts of happiness. She was thrilled to see them all, but it quickly became overwhelming. So much so that she was actually relieved when Dr. Pearse arrived and sternly insisted that everyone leave.

They all marched out the door calling farewells and promising to be back soon. Finally, there was only Dr. Pearse, Sophia, and Devon. The doctor turned to the duke but one glare from Devon had him clearing his throat and pretending he wasn't there. Sophia managed to roll her eyes, earning herself a wink for her troubles.

"You're quite flushed, Miss Templeworth," Dr. Pearse claimed. "Are you too hot?"

A chuckle from where Devon stood was proof positive that he knew what that wink had done to her, and she glared at him but immediately winced as even that hurt.

"The pain will be a rather close companion for a time, I'm afraid," Dr. Pearse said sympathetically patting her hand until a growl from Devon had him swiftly removing it. "I think perhaps some laudanum to help you sleep. That really is the best way to recover."

But she didn't want to sleep again. She wanted to find out what had happened whilst she'd been unconscious. She wanted to know if everyone in Halton considered her to be engaged to Devon. But Dr. Pearse was already handing her a draught.

"I'm not sure if this is a good idea," she groused.

"Dr. Pearse, I had hoped to speak to Miss Templeworth about a rather important issue." She stared at Devon, who stared at the doctor, who swallowed loudly.

"It would be best for Miss Templeworth's recovery to take the draught, Your Grace."

Devon sighed, regret clear in his eyes as he smiled at her. "Of course, doctor. Her recovery is more important than anything else."

She took the medicine, wincing as she swallowed it down.

Almost immediately the effects started to work, and her eyes grew heavier and heavier. She was vaguely aware of someone leaving and an inexplicable panic clawed at her. "Devon," she managed. "Stay."

There was a moment of silence and then she felt the mattress dip and she was surrounded by his scent. "I'm not going anywhere, lass," he whispered. "I'll stay right by your side for as long as you'll have me."

Chapter Twenty-Six

C HRISTMAS EVE HAD dawned, cold and frosty as it should be. Sophia had been alone for what felt like hours as she watched the sky through a slit in the curtains turn blue to pink to black.

It was a beautiful, starry night and she was heartily sick of it. Not only because she'd been staring out the same window for days now but because now that she was awake more than she was asleep, Devon had returned to sleeping in his own chambers at night. During the day he split his time between sitting with her and playing with the children or bonding with her family, at least according to her sisters who also sat with her every day.

"He's so huge that they've taken to climbing him like a tree," Hope had quipped. "Don't worry, little sister. I'm sure when you're recovered, you'll get your turn."

In the midst of Elodie scolding Hope and Francesca snorting, they'd told her about what had happened the night of her accident. How Christian, Gideon, and Adam had all tried to force Devon to insist they marry. How he'd refused to take her choices from her. And how he'd kept a vigil by her bedside morning, noon, and night. Never leaving, never giving up on her. Refusing to think the worst even when the others couldn't seem to help it.

"I thought he might go mad with the worry, Sophia," Elodie had said to her just last night. "I don't think he'll ever let you out of his sight now."

Sophia lay there ruminating over her sisters' assurances. They had no reason to lie. And she thought she'd seen evidence of affection, perhaps even love from Devon ever since she'd woken up. Yet he hadn't once broached the subject of his proposal. Hadn't even talked about that awful night save to apologize over and over and over about causing it to happen. No matter how often she told him she didn't blame him, she saw how it haunted him. Even now that he slept and ate and no longer looked like a ghost, it haunted him.

Perhaps with time he would stop blaming himself. The problem was that she had no idea if he expected her to be around when he did.

When he'd first gotten her to agree to his scheme, he asked her to give him until he was leaving to make a decision. He'd said he wanted to return to Scotland with her on his arm. But he was leaving after Christmas, and he hadn't mentioned it again.

It was as though he'd quite forgotten. Or maybe he just didn't want her anymore. Maybe she'd ruined it all by overreacting that night and causing such chaos, such concern among them all. Or maybe now that he'd grown closer to the children, he'd simply decided that he didn't need a wife. At least not in a hurry. No, he had the time now to fall in love she supposed.

Well, that was fine. If he'd changed his mind, then that was just fine. She didn't need him if he didn't need her. And if it felt as though her heart were breaking, well, that was just a leftover injury from her accident. That made perfect sense. She had never pined for a man before, and she wasn't about to start now.

There was a sharp rap on the door, and she recognized it as Devon's. Schooling her features into a mask of indifference she called out for him to enter. And then there he was. His smile was a thing of beauty, those dimples that somehow made him even more handsome making an appearance.

"Good evening, lass," he said. "How are you feeling this evening?" He strode over and dropped a chaste kiss on her brow, as had become his wont.

"I'm fine," she answered a little stiffly. Because she *was* fine. Or she would be. She would force herself to be.

Devon straightened up and studied her intently for a moment before he moved to take his usual seat by her bed. "The children are excited about tomorrow," he said with a smile. "Heather was insisting on bringing you some holly before bed. She doesn't think it's fair for you to miss out on the decorations you worked so hard to procure. I managed to convince her to wait until tomorrow morning."

She managed a smile at the idea of little Heather demanding to come in and decorate her room. But it soon disappeared. He'd barely spent any time with her today, and she hated how much she ached for him considering he seemed to have lost interest.

"Perhaps you feel able to leave your bedchamber for a spell?" Devon asked, leaning forward, elbows on his knees as he gazed at her.

"I'd *love* to," she said straight away. "Did Dr. Pearse say I could?"

"He took a little persuading," Devon said darkly, and she felt a twinge of pity for the poor doctor. Devon had had the man harassed since her accident. Especially in the first few days, her sisters had told her. Cheska took great delight in telling her that he'd run from the house crying the night of her accident with Devon on his heels like the devil himself.

"But he agreed that you were likely to start throwing and breaking things if you didn't break out soon. I'm allowed to carry you to wherever you want to go as long as it's in the house and for no more than an hour."

"Wow," she drawled sarcastically. "How will I contain my excitement?"

Devon's lips quirked into a crooked smile. "I've missed that feistiness," he drawled setting gooseflesh breaking out all over her body. He dropped his eyes to the exposed skin of her decolletage, his smile becoming a smugly satisfied smirk as he witnessed his effect on her. "And I am counting down the days until I can show you how much."

Despite her confusion, despite convincing herself that he'd lost interest in her, those silly butterflies awoke from hibernation and burst into movement in her belly. And though she shouldn't, she found herself raising a brow at him. "And how do you propose to show me, Your Grace?"

His groan skittered along her nerves, and he stood to lean over her, his face dropping toward hers. "Don't tempt me, lass. I need to behave myself. For now."

She didn't know quite how to respond so she dropped her gaze to the coverlet, hating the heat creeping up her cheeks.

"Up you come, temptress," Devon said, scooping her into his arms. Sophia screeched and threw her arms around his neck, delighting in his husky laugh, nuzzling into his chest. She didn't want this to be the last chance she'd get to do this but knew there was a possibility that it would be. So, she was making the most of it.

The house was oddly quiet as Devon made his way to the library, acting as though she weighed nothing at all. It felt so good to be out of her bedchamber, even if it was in her night rail with her hair unbound.

This morning, Elodie had helped her bathe, and she had felt so much better as Hope had brushed out her hair by the fire. Francesca had simply lain on the freshly changed bedding claiming that she couldn't possibly help in her condition.

"Where is everyone?" she wondered aloud. "I thought the house would be a flurry of activity to prepare for tomorrow."

"I believe everyone retired to the nursery wing," he said smoothly. "The children will be impossible to settle, so it sounds like quite a party up there."

"You didn't want to join them?" she asked quietly.

He looked down at her, his eyes boring into her soul.

"No," he said. "If I only get an hour with you, I want you all to myself."

The library door was closed when they reached it, so Devon

transferred all her weight to one arm then reached out to turn the doorknob. He pushed it open, and Sophia gasped as she took in the sight of what seemed like thousands of candles lighting on every surface.

And there by the fire was a bottle of Adam's good brandy and two glasses. Sophia felt her eyes smart as she took it all in. She turned to look up at him. "You did all this?" He nodded, watching her face closely. "Why?" she gasped.

He didn't answer straight away, instead moving to the chaise and setting her down gently. Her ribs were still tender, so he spent some time piling up cushions under and around her until she, laughing, told him to stop fussing like a mother hen. When he decided she was comfortable, he turned and poured a finger of brandy into each tumbler then settled himself on the edge of the chaise.

"A toast," he said softly. "To having your beautiful eyes opened and on me again."

Sophia's heart melted at the words, and she threw back the contents of her glass lest she do something foolish like blubber all over him and demand to know why he didn't seem to want her for a wife anymore.

"You asked me why I did all this," Devon said, waving a hand around the room. He reached out and plucked her empty glass from her hand placing it alongside his own on the table then turned back to gaze into her eyes. "It's because I asked you a question, Sophia. And the answer is due."

DEVON WORKED DESPERATELY hard to keep his nerve, even though his heart was hammering in his chest. He watched his words sink in, watched Sophia's eyes widen as she registered their meaning and once again, a wave of relief so intense that it almost floored him swept through him.

He still couldn't believe how close he'd come to losing her. Still awoke in the night sometimes reaching for her as though he were watching her fall all over again. When that happened, he paced down the corridor to her room and sat there all night long, just in case she cried out for someone. Just to make sure she was in there and safe.

But now that he knew she was on the way to recovery, he couldn't wait any longer. He wanted an answer to the question that had been burning in his heart since he'd asked her. But before she answered him, he needed to finally be honest and tell her what was in his heart. He wanted her to know why he wanted her. The real reason.

But before he did that, there was one more thing he wanted to do, just in case it was the last time he got to do it. Leaning forward, he captured her lips with his own. He didn't deepen it as he wanted to, didn't grab the nape of her neck, and pull her toward him like he ached to do. He'd just needed to taste her. Just once.

Pulling back, he ran a thumb over her cheek then opened his mouth to finally speak the words that had been building up inside him. But before he could, the door burst open, and her entire bloody family poured into the room.

"I think we're too early." Good God, her sisters' whispers could be heard all in the way in Scotland.

Chapter Twenty-Seven

S OPHIA'S STOMACH DROPPED to her toes at the interruption. She'd never learn, it seemed. Because she had once again gotten her hopes up and now, she was sitting here disappointed.

"You all need to leave."

Her eyes snapped up to Devon's face, her jaw dropping open in shock.

"This is my house," Francesca said stubbornly.

"That's my sister." Hope sounded indignant.

"My love, perhaps we should give them some space."

"Hope, darling, this seems as though it should be private."

She heard her sisters argue with their respective husbands, but it was all in the background because her entire being was focused on Devon.

They bickered back and forth for a time before Elodie's smooth, ladylike tone interrupted. "Let's all leave them to it."

Hope and Francesca tried to argue but within seconds Elodie had them rounded up and out the door. The soft click of it shutting sounded loud as a gunshot to Sophia's ears.

"You know, the fact that I'm still willing to marry you even though I'll be getting all of that in the deal should go a long way in my favor." Her heart stopped dead in her chest.

"A-are you saying that you still want to marry me?"

He looked at her as though she was crazy. "Of course, I do," he said. "Why would you think I didn't?"

"Well, you haven't exactly been dying to bring it up," she said, feeling a little defensive. "So, I thought maybe you'd changed your mind. Decided that you didn't need a wife to help with the children."

"Ah," he said, nodding solemnly. "Well, now that you mention it, you're absolutely right. I have decided that I don't need a wife to help with the children."

"Oh." She couldn't give in to the pain trying to claim her. She simply couldn't. *This is fine,* she told herself. *It's fine.* "Well, I-I think it's good that we know now h-how we both feel and, and we can part ways as friends."

She was going to fall apart. She could feel it in the very fiber of her being. The heartache was threatening to overwhelm her, and she needed to get away but she was stuck. Her legs wouldn't carry her all the way up to her bedchamber. She was at his mercy completely. She would never again be held in his arms, never again feel his mouth pressed to hers, never again know the joy he awoke in her body.

"That's just it," he said, his tone so gentle that it made her want to burst into tears. "I'm afraid that you don't know how I feel, and I don't think parting as friends is on the cards for us."

"Why not?" she demanded, and though she tried to keep her tone stern, she found that she couldn't meet his eye. The idea of not even having him as a friend was anathema to her. It would hurt but never seeing him again would surely hurt a lot more.

When he didn't immediately answer her, she was forced to look into his eyes. And her breathing hitched at the look in them. Slowly, he reached out and grasped the hands that she'd had firmly clasped together.

"Because I want so much more from you than friendship, lass. I meant what I said, I don't want to marry you for the sake of the children. I want to marry you because—because I love you, Sophia Templeworth. I am so very in love with you. And I cannot imagine a moment of my life that isn't spent with you."

For a brief moment his words didn't sink in. But when they

did, an elation unlike anything she'd ever known burst inside her, lighting her up like fireworks, and she promptly burst into tears. Not the pretty kind like Elodie cried. But heaving sobs that no doubt made her face blotchy.

Devon looked horrified, and he moved from the chaise to drop to his haunches beside her. "Please don't cry," he begged. "I ask nothing more of you than what you're willing to give, Sophia. You do not have to love me as I love you. I'm not even sure it's possible for you to love me that much." His self-deprecating smile was almost her undoing and her heart ached with the love that was overflowing, threatening to consume her. She wanted to throw her arms around him. Tell him that of course she loved him that much. How could she not when it seemed as though he'd been made for her? But he wasn't done. Outside the door there was the distinct sound of gasps and I told you so's" but it was easy to block it all out in favor of the man before her.

"I want to marry you because I have no idea how to live without you anymore. But I understand that I'm reneging on what we agreed to," he said. "And I'll take you in any capacity I can get. So, if you agree, even if it's for Heather and Finn, then you'll still make me the happiest man in Christendom. So, will you do it, lass? Will you marry me? For them, if not for anything else."

Sophia had lost all ability to speak. For a wild moment, she wondered if she was dreaming. If the laudanum had caused her to have an elaborate, wonderful dream. But she could feel the heat from the fire, and she could hear her interfering sisters outside, and she knew that it was real. Impossibly wonderful as it seemed, it was real.

"No, Devon," she said softly, "I won't marry you for the children." She saw the look of pain that flashed through his eyes, and she knew then that she would never willingly cause him pain again. She would never allow him to doubt, not for one moment, how much she loved him. "I will marry you," she said softly, leaning forward to touch his cheek. "I will marry you because I love you so much, I cannot imagine anything worse than not sharing every second of my life with you. I will love those children as though they were my own, but I will only be your wife because of *you* and how much I need you in my life."

His smile was the most beautiful thing in the world, and he grabbed hold of her face to pull her in for a soul searing kiss.

Once again, the door to the library burst open but this time, she didn't care that her family descended on them screeching and applauding and calling for champagne. There was much back-clapping and kissing. The children ran wild as they explained to Finn and Heather what it was to be a cousin.

And through it all, Devon kept hold of Sophia's hand, his smile promising her the world. And she thought to herself that maybe being a duchess wouldn't be so bad.

Chapter Twenty-Eight

"A JUNE WEDDING would have been more suitable. You could have been married in front of the entire *ton*. It's not every day that a duke marries you know."

Sophia had stopped listening to her mother ages ago. She didn't listen when Mama tried to get her to wait and have a wedding with hundreds of people. She didn't listen when she tried to insist that they hold off until distant relatives she'd never heard of could come and witness her become a duchess. And she didn't listen when Mama told everyone in Halton that the prince himself might attend.

Lord, when Devon had let slip that he knew the Prince Regent, it had been one of the worst days of Sophia's life. Ever since then Mama had been even more impossible than usual, and it had driven her up the walls. So much so that she'd ended up staying at Heywood to get ready for the wedding.

Christmas had come and gone, the celebration one of the most joyous Sophia had ever had. And even though she'd still been recovering, even though she still *was* recovering, she had enjoyed every second of it.

There'd been gifts and music and laughter. But most importantly, Devon had been right there by her side.

And now, on the eve of Twelfth Night, she was finally ready to make him hers forever.

"Mama, Kit is ready to start," Hope appeared in the door of

the bedchamber, winking at Sophia. Gideon's brother had been only too happy to officiate the wedding and had promised that he'd keep it short so Mama wouldn't have time to put in too much of a performance.

Though she'd wanted to keep the wedding small, it wasn't really surprising that the entirety of Halton had turned out for it. After all, not only was the last of the notorious Templeworth girls marrying, but it wasn't every day a duke got married in their tiny little hamlet.

The doors to the small church opened and she immediately sought Devon out. He looked glorious—there really was no other word for it. He towered over poor Kit, looking like a fearsome highland warrior of old. But when his gaze found hers, there was nothing but tenderness and love in their dark depths. And suddenly, she couldn't wait to get up that aisle and marry the man she never knew she needed.

"MY MOTHER THINKS we should have waited and married in June."

Devon rolled his eyes and pulled his wife, his *wife*, closer to his body making sure to be careful with her as they danced. They weren't staying long since she was still recuperating and he was quite simply desperate to get her alone. In fact, the recuperating part was a blatant lie since she'd been fine for weeks, but the opportunity had presented itself and he was taking it.

Tomorrow they would leave for the Continent. Heather and Finn were beside themselves with excitement at the idea of spending four weeks with their cousins at Brentford. And his mother was excited to get back to Farnshire and begin her move to the dowager house so that Castle would be ready for Sophia to become mistress.

"Your mother can keep her opinions to herself," he growled

in her ear, delighting in her shiver of need. He'd been climbing the walls while waiting for the wedding to be planned. His new brothers-in-law taking great delight in keeping a close eye on him so he couldn't get his bride on her own.

But now she was his wife, and he could spend as much time alone with her as he wanted. That one thought snapped the last vestiges of his control and without even waiting for the waltz to be finished, he grabbed hold of her and practically ran from the ballroom of Adam's manor house and straight to her bedchamber.

He ignored the cackles from his sisters-in-law and the knowing smirks from the other lords. And when he finally got her to her bedchamber, he locked the door and pulled her into his arms.

"Do you know what the best thing about a winter wedding is?" he asked against her lips as he tore her dress from her body.

"What's that?" she gasped making light work of divesting him of his own clothing.

When he'd stripped her bare, he hefted her into his arms, groaning as she wrapped those incredible legs around his waist.

Carrying her to the bed, he loomed over her and hovered at her entrance as he finally answered her question.

"I get to keep you warm," he answered before finally driving himself home.

Epilogue

"**H**EATHER, FINN, THEY'RE here."

Sophia laughed at the thunderous sound of feet on the stairs. Even at the age of twelve and eight they got just as excited when people came to visit as they always had.

Devon appeared from the drawing room carrying Duncan in one arm and Celia in the other. The twins were a handful, but he was infinitely patient with them. Bending down, he pressed a tender kiss on her lips and there went the riot of butterflies, even after all this time. He winked down at her because he knew what he did to her. She'd told him often enough.

The carriages stopped on the gravel driveway of the castle and one after the other the doors opened and people spilled out. The children, of course, congregated at once, even Duncan and Celia who were helped along by Finn and Heather.

Sophia tore down the steps and into the arms of her sisters while Devon led Christian, Gideon, and Adam into the house, no doubt planning on drinking more than one bottle of brandy.

"I always enjoy visiting Farnshire," Francesca said. "Marcus is determined to learn to ice fish this year, so warn Devon, won't you? And knowing Madelene she won't be far behind," she added, smiling indulgently at her children.

"Let them all fish," Hope said with a wave of her hand. "It will give us a chance to catch up properly. Did you hear the pig farmer finally married?"

Sophia gasped. "Who on earth would marry him?"

"Perhaps he's grown nicer," Elodie offered.

"Hmm. And perhaps his pigs have started to fly," snorted Francesca.

"Dr. Pearse found himself an Italian wife, too."

"Did he really?"

"I'm glad. I hope she has nice ankles, he has a penchant for them does he not?"

The sisters continued to gossip and laugh as they walked arm in arm up the steps of the castle. They swept into the drawing room, Elodie going straight into Christian's arms where he stood by the fireplace. Hope sitting on Gideon's lap, and Francesca throwing herself onto the chaise beside Adam, throwing her legs onto his lap. Sophia drifted to where Devon was busy pouring brandy into eight tumblers, determined to get Elodie to like it, since everyone else did.

He immediately set the decanter down and pulled her toward him for a brazen, heated kiss. "I can't wait to warm you up later," he whispered in her ear before handing out tumblers to everyone then taking Sophia's hand in his own.

"To Christmas," he raised his glass. "To family. And to the Templeworth girls and the men who've survived them."

About the Author

Nadine Millard is an international best-selling author hailing from Dublin, Ireland.

Having studied and then worked in law for a number of years, Nadine began to live her dream of writing when she had the first of her three children.

She released her debut novel in 2014 and has been writing ever since.

When she's not writing she can be found reading anything she can get her hands on, ferrying her three children to school and clubs, spoiling her cat, her dog, and snatching time with her long-suffering husband!

You can find out all about Nadine and her books at www.nadinemillard.com.